Ctrl Z

The Do Over

Stone

pdmac

Ctrl Z, The Do Over Stone is a work of fiction. Though actual locations and persons may be mentioned, they are used in a fictitious manner and the events and occurrences were created/invented in the mind and imagination of the author. Any other resemblance to actual persons, living or dead, events, or locales is purely coincidental.

Published by Trimble Hollow Press, Acworth, Georgia

ISBN: 978-1-946495-07-5

eISBN: 978-1-946495-06-8

Cover design by Rebecacovers and Trimble Hollow Concepts

for Terri Lynn

my Soulmate and Best Friend

ALSO BY PDMAC

Wyvern Master Chronicles
The Sixth Kingdom
A Spy in the Court
Raising the Death
Wizard King

Misfits of Gambria
Berserker of Gambria
The Voice of Thunder
Ghost in the Desert
A Wizard of Sorts
No rest for the Wicked
A Noble Rebellion
No Loose Ends
Quest for a Throne
A Queen Most Evil
Warlord of Gambria

Viking Time Travel Romance
Beyond Her Touch
Hidden in Time

Bridge Quest: A GameLit Adventure Series

Bridge Quest

Orc's Bane

Lord of Innis Torr

Steampunk Western: Tombstone Series

Fool's Gold

An Ounce of Lead

Dystopian

Rebirth of Angels

Dragons of Isentol

Throne of Deceit

Runemarked

Empire of Serpents

A Time Travel Novella

Ctrl Z: The Do Over Stone

Poetry

a young man no more

Chapter 1

Mark sat on the park bench adding up the number of ways he hoped she'd die. His favorite so far was abduction by terrorists followed by horrific torture. She would be blindfolded and bloody, kneeling on the concrete floor as the terrorists postured before the camera, threatening to cut off her head.

Gazing out over the lake, watching the herons glide in wide-winged flight then settle among the cat of nine tails made him think a plane crash might be good, a long plummeting descent from 30,000 feet, her hands clutching the armrests and the oxygen mask dangling just beyond her reach.

On the water in the distance, two women in kayaks skirted the shore as they headed to the northern part of the wide lake where the river snaked its way from the mountains more than a hundred miles away. The music theme from *Jaws* echoed and he envisioned her paddling furiously as the shark fin cut through the tranquil water, her cries of terror unheeded.

The day was lazily warm and the scent of freshwater and flowers and trees would normally have invigorated Mark, but today was not one of those days. Normally, instead of sitting here in the early afternoon, he would be at work as an insurance adjuster. Well, that wasn't really accurate. He didn't adjust anything except maybe the thermostat in the office when Sheila complained it was too hot, which was most of the time because she was continually having hot flashes. Her condition reduced the temperature in the office to that of a meat freezer.

While most of his peers were content to silently endure the frigid temps by wearing enough clothes to climb Mount Everest, all the while directing hushed obscenities at the boss who was both impervious and uncaring to their plight, Mark made the fatal error of giving voice concerning his shivering and numb fingers and hands.

"How am I supposed to enter data if I can't move my fingers to type?" he had exclaimed, sitting at his desk, his hands hovering over the keyboard.

Of course it was an exaggeration because he could move his fingers, awkwardly, but they did move. Hearing his frustration Sheila emerged from her office and curled a lip before acidly observing, "You don't like working here?"

"That's not what I said," he snapped before realizing his tone was less than respectful.

Sheila, a plump martinet in pinstriped pant suit, stiffened to full height, which wasn't much taller than the filing cabinets in her office.

"Then what did you say?" Her voice was colder than the room.

"What I said was it's so cold in here that my hands won't cooperate. How can we work when it's freezing in here?" The words poured out before he had a chance to stop himself.

Sheila stood imperiously gazing out over the low-walled cubicles where the heads of her subordinates popped up like so many prairie dogs.

"Who else thinks it's too cold in here?" she demanded, her tone daring anyone to join Mark's doomed crusade.

As the prairie dog heads popped back down behind the safety of their cubicle walls in unison, Mark realized he had just been offered up as a sacrifice to appease the goddess Sheila.

"Well," Sheila cruelly intoned. "Looks like you're the only one who feels this way, Mister Clum." She drew out his name in one long syllable. "That's one thing I've noticed about you," she continued, her voice carrying out over the entire office area of twenty cubicles. "You're a slacker, a complainer, and it shows in the poor quality of your work."

"That's bullsh –" Mark exploded before clamping his lips tight and silently castigating himself because he knew better, especially as his desk was in line of sight of the witch and she could see everything he did.

"What did you say?" She glared at him.

"I said that's not true," he lamely replied.

"That's NOT what I heard. Your language is entirely inappropriate."

"I didn't say anything inappropriate," he objected.

"Are you contradicting me?" she demanded, an eyebrow raised.

"If that's what you call it," Mark answered, suddenly emboldened.

Startled at the response, her nostrils flaring, Sheila's ice eyes locked onto him. "How dare you be impertinent with me."

"Impertinent?" he sniffed. "I'm surprised you know the meaning of the word. This has nothing to do with impertinence and everything to do with working conditions. Why don't you wear a swimsuit or something and let the rest

3

of us shed some of our winter clothing? Though seeing you in a swimsuit would probably give me nightmares."

As soon as he said it, he knew he would regret it.

"How dare you," she exploded. "Your language and attitude are entirely inappropriate and will not be tolerated. You are dismissed as an employee from this company. You will leave immediately or I will have you physically escorted out of the building. Don't even think about dawdling to collect your personal things. They will be delivered to the address H.R. has on file. Now go." She lifted an imperious hand and pointed to the door.

"You're firing me?" Mark responded, his voice rising.

"As is obvious," she declared and turned her back to him. Striding back into her office, she made a show of sliding calmly into the chair behind her desk and directing her attention to the computer screen as though nothing significant had happened.

Mark wanted to say something clever to her, but nothing came to mind. Turning, he saw a few heads of his coworkers pop up, giving him a universal 'That was dumb' stare before popping back down.

Shoving his chair into the desk, he called out, "You're all cowards," as he stormed off.

The failure in his quest for the working conditions of the little man led him to the park bench where he now sat, licking the wounds of his vanity. It was as he was deliberating his next move that the man sat down next to him. Turning to look at him, Mark gave him an exasperated frown and scooted an inch away as an overt statement that he had been sitting there first.

The man was impeccably dressed in a three-piece business suit. His wavy dark blond hair was perfectly coiffured and he wore designer sunglasses. He was trim and had that chiseled face advertisers love to exploit. He looked to be late forties or early fifties, a successful man in his prime.

He slowly twirled something in his hands, and Mark looked down to see a smooth stone that one could find in any river. It was uniformly colored a blue-gray.

"You look like a man who could use this," the man said, staring straight ahead.

"Use what?"

"The stone."

"The stone?"

"Yes."

"Why would I need a stone?"

"It can help."

"Help what?" Mark said, wondering why all the wackos in the universe seemed to be drawn to him. It was like he had the word 'SUCKER' stamped on his forehead.

"With whatever problem you're having." The man turned to look at him, his eyes betraying neither friendship nor animosity. "I saw you sitting here and knew you had problems and I said to myself, that boy there could use this."

Mark shook his head and sniffed in disdain. "What's a rock going to do to help me?"

"It's not a rock, it's a stone, a very *special* stone," he said.

"And what's this very *special* stone supposed to do for me?" Mark looked askance at him, hoping the man wasn't going to launch into some absurd marketing pitch for the latest fad.

The man's head did a slow swivel, casting covert glances at those nearby then leaned towards Mark.

"It's a 'Do Over' stone."

"A what?"

"A 'Do Over' stone."

"A 'do over' stone," Mark loudly repeated.

"Shhhh," the man cautioned, waving a hand at him. "Not so loud. You want everyone to hear us?"

"Sorry," he replied without conviction. "So what does a 'do over' stone do?"

The man frowned at Mark's obtuseness. "It lets you 'do over' things you wish you could do over."

For some reason this struck Mark as funny and he smirked. "Like Ctrl Z."

"Ctrl Z?" the man repeated, puzzled.

"Yeah, you know," Mark replied, giving him a quizzical look. "On the keyboard. When you want to erase something and do it over, you hit the Ctrl key and then the 'Z' key. It erases what you just typed and you can do it over. Don't you ever use a computer?"

"Of course, but I have others type my correspondence," he replied then smiled. "Ctrl Z... I like the analogy. However, this is much better," he winked.

Mark snickered. "OK. So how's it work?"

The man's eyes lit up. "All you have to do is rub the stone and say the words 'Do over' out loud and whatever you wanted to do over, you get to do again. But there's a time limit. You can't redo things more than an hour ago. Also, you can control how far back you go within the hour just by thinking where you want to be."

A wide grin split Mark's face. "Just rub the stone and say the words and poof, I get to redo whatever it is?"

"That's it."

Still grinning, Mark gave him the once over. "If the stone works so well, why do you want to get rid of it?"

The man leaned back with confident aplomb. "I've made my millions. I'm at a point where my money makes money. It's time to pass the stone along, let someone else in on the rewards." He narrowed his gaze at Mark. "But I warn you. You are responsible for the choices you make, good or bad. Remember, the stone can only undo what has happened within the past hour. After that, you live with the choices you make, so make them wisely. Often we realize our poor choices too late."

Mark eyed him with a mocking smile. "So you now want to give me the stone?"

"Yes. You look like a man who is responsible." He turned to look out over the lake. "But more importantly, you look like a man who has just lost his job."

Mark's smile vanished. "That's none of your business."

"I meant no offense, my friend." He sighed and ruefully nodded then stared into the distance. "I too suffered the same fate. Sitting here on this very same park bench, years ago, I too pondered what I was going to do with my life. That's when I received the Do Over stone. The man who gave it to me was well-dressed and refined. 'I've made my fortune,' he said. 'It's time to pass on the stone. You look like a man who is responsible.' I didn't believe him at first, not until he showed me his car and chauffeur."

"So what happened?" Mark asked, beginning to enjoy the tale, no matter how absurd it was.

"He handed me the stone and departed. I never met him again. The last I heard, he was living on some tropical island he owned, with all the modern conveniences without the trappings of crowds and unwanted persons."

"Sounds marvelous." Mark leaned back, crossing one leg over the other.

"Yes it does." The man exhaled a deep breath. "And now it's time to pass on the stone." He held it out in his hand.

"That's OK," Mark said holding up his hands. "You keep it. You might still need it."

The man gave him a sympathetic smile. "I understand. I had the same reaction. Try it first. Take the stone and return to your place of employment. Rub the stone and repeat the words."

"I'm not going back there," Mark retorted. "I was fired."

"I understand," he patiently replied. "If you were fired, what do you have to lose?"

"They won't even let me back in the building," he pointed out.

"They will this time."

"I'm not going to make a fool of myself for your pleasure," he huffed and started to stand when the man grabbed his arm.

"What do you have to lose? Pride? Who cares about pride other than you? Just try it. If it doesn't work, you can give the stone back to me and you've lost nothing."

Jerking his arm from the man's surprisingly strong grip, Mark's overwhelming urge was to walk away from the crazy man, no matter how well dressed he was. Yet a part of him wanted to go back and at least get one last word in before he was physically tossed out the doors. For some reason, the vision of berating Sheila with some choice words before being tossed out the doors had a twisted attraction. Besides, once he as outside again, he could finally get rid of the pesky man.

The man watched him silently deliberate then stuck out a hand. "My name's Nathan Blaylock. You can ask around and you'll find out that I'm rich. You give this a try. If it doesn't work, I'll buy you dinner at the most expensive restaurant in the city."

He handed Mark a business card artfully engraved with his name, telephone numbers, websites, and the words 'CEO Blaylock, Ltd."

Mark blinked in recognition. "I have heard of you."

"What have you got to lose? Either it works or you get a free dinner."

Mark studied him a moment longer, wondering if he was being set up for some stupid game that someone was filming from some hidden spot. Yet he reasoned what would most likely happen was that he would never make it past the security guards and he could simply turn around and give the stone back.

"OK. I'll give it a try." He held out his hand and took the small stone, shoving it into his pocket.

"A couple of things to remember," Nathan said. "First, the stone only works for you. You can't control what happens to others. For example, if you see a plane crashing, you can't change it because it doesn't immediately affect you."

"Unless I'm on it," he pointed out.

"Yes, unless you're on it," Nathan agreed.

"What else?"

"Remember the hour time limit. Even if it's one second past an hour, it won't work. All you have to do is imagine where you were at some point in time of that hour and you will be transported back to that moment."

Standing on the wide pavement outside his office building, Nathan cast a sideward glance at him. "It's not been more than an hour, right? The stone won't work if it's been more than an hour," he fretted.

"It's been about forty minutes," Mark reassured him, staring at the main revolving door, wondering just how quickly he would be ejected.

"You need to get going if it's going to work."

"I'm going," he replied. With a deep breath, he pushed through the revolving door.

He was surprised when the front desk personnel in the lobby looked up and paid him no mind. He was again astounded when no one paid him more than cursory attention as he rode the elevator up to his work floor. He was further amazed when he timidly opened the door to the cubicles of his office area and no one thought to give him a second glance.

Standing in the doorway, he reached into his pocket and rubbed the stone, pronouncing the words, "Do over."

The room went into a blurred swirl and in an instant, he was at his desk, his numb fingers hovering over the keyboard.

"My God," he exclaimed. His hand went to his pocket and he felt the reassuring lump of stone. "It worked."

Sheila strutted out the door to her office. "What's going on?" she demanded, giving him a cold stare.

"Nothing, you fat bitch," he grinned.

"What?" she sputtered, her eyes bolting wide in anger.

"Uh... uh." Mark quickly reached into his pocket and rubbed the stone. "Do over."

There was a flash and Sheila again strutted out the door to her office. "What's going on?" she demanded, giving him the exact cold stare of only a moment ago.

"Nothing," he laughed, "you ugly slut."

"What?" she snapped.

"Do over."

For the next five minutes, Mark had Sheila reappear at the door while he hurled wild and vivid epithets at her, all the while berating her for her incompetence. His laughter grew with each verbal assault until he was shaking uncontrollably.

Finally, Sheila emerged from the office and saw his mirth. "What's so funny?" she demanded.

"Nothing," he replied, using the heels of his palms to wipe away the tears of laughter. "I just love working here."

Sheila's demeanor morphed from stern scowl to a stern smile. "See?" she called out to the rest of the workers. "This is what I'm talking about. Mark has the right attitude, upbeat and energetic. You all can take a lesson from him."

"I'll be right back," Mark said.

"Where are you going?" she said with a frown.

"Just need to use the restroom. Then I can't wait to get back to work."

"Fine," she said with an approving nod. "When you get back, stop by my office. I've got a special project I want you to work on."

"Yes Mam," he replied with a dedicated grin.

Bounding out the door and down the hall to the stairs in the outer stairwells because the elevators were too slow, he emerged in the lobby then swung through the revolving door. Once outside, he was disappointed when Nathan was nowhere to be found. After a few minutes, he gave up his search and returned to the office, his happiness overshadowing the mild disappointment of not thanking his benefactor.

Mark's fortune improved dramatically as several days later, Sheila promoted him to her deputy. Still, Mark took to the daily joy of deriding and mocking his boss, each time laughing uproariously at the ability to give vent to his thoughts without repercussion. Evenings found him at home researching new and clever attacks. Yet, all in all, he was thoroughly enjoying the job. He even got Sheila to increase the temperature in the office area.

One afternoon, he waited in line at the bank, musing on his good luck. Life was certainly improving. All he needed now was a girlfriend and more money in the bank… yes, more money in the bank. It was then an idea crept into the edges of his consciousness and pushed itself forward.

When his turn came, he told the cashier, a matronly woman in her mid-forties, his account number then asked, "How much do I have in my checking account?"

"You have thirteen hundred dollars in your account," she replied.

"I'd like to withdraw two hundred dollars in cash, please."

"How would you like that?"

"Two one hundreds would be fine."

The woman typed in the transaction, pulled open the cash drawer and selected two one-hundred-dollar bills, counted them again and handed the bills to him.

Folding the bills and stuffing them into his pocket, he rubbed the stone and said, "Do over."

The room whirled and settled. Reaching into his pocket, he felt the crisp bills of the two hundred dollars.

"How much do I have my checking account, please?"

"You have thirteen hundred dollars in your account," the matronly cashier replied.

"I'd like to withdraw five hundred dollars in cash, please."

By the time he concluded his transactions, Mark's pockets bulged with wads of cash. After the last 'Do over,' Mark decided to quit while he was ahead.

Giving the cashier his account number, he said, "I'd like to make a deposit into my checking account."

"And how much did you want to deposit today?" she asked.

Mark unburdened his pockets and counted out his cash, keeping a few hundred for himself. "Make that eight thousand and six hundred dollars."

The cashier accepted the bills, recounted them and entered the amount into Mark's account before handing him a receipt for the deposit.

Glancing down at the receipt as he walked through the foyer, Mark grinned when he saw that his account had grown to almost ten thousand dollars.

His first urge was to tell his apartment neighbor Kyle of his success. Kyle worked as a stocker at the local grocery store. He and Mark shared a common bond in their passion for Cosplay. Kyle's preferred costume was Hellboy while Mark gravitated towards Captain America.

Yet the more Mark thought about it, the less inclined he was to explain how he came by his newfound wealth. He was not ready to share the power of the 'Do over' stone. Perhaps when he had everything he wanted, then he might be ready to part with the stone. An idea germinated and he smiled, for it was a way to demonstrate his good fortune without actually revealing the stone.

"You wanna do what?" Kyle frowned when Mark announced his intention.

"We're going to the horse races," he replied with a confident grin as he studied Kyle's latest Hellboy costume. "You're getting better with the horn nubs," he complimented.

"Thanks. I don't know a thing about horse racing," Kyle responded, reaching up and adjusting a nub.

"Me neither," Mark said, "but I'm feeling lucky."

"The last time you felt lucky was when you tried to hook up with that chick dressed as Vampirella."

"She was hot."

"Yeah," Kyle snickered, "so hot you got burned. Shot down. Burst into flames."

"Yeah, well, my luck is about to change. You coming with me or not? It's not like you got anywhere else you have to be and it's really cheap to get in."

"When?"

"Saturday."

"Yeah, OK."

Standing in line at the betting window, Kyle leaned in. "You didn't tell me you were going to bet money."

"It's the only currency they take," Mark deadpanned then stepped to the window. "Race one, $2 to win on number 7." Mark placed the two singles on the counter and received his ticket.

While most folks made their way to the stands, he led the way over to join a small group of bettors watching a monitor that was mounted high on the wall.

"Let's see how we do," he said, staring up at the TV.

The horse gates opened and the thoroughbreds leaped forward. Those watching began urging their picks to run faster. Even Kyle began cheering and encouraging, surprised that Mark stood calmly watching, uninvolved.

As the horses crossed the finish line, the announcer called out, "It's Arrogant Beauty by half a length, followed by Starlight Mist and Dreamweaver in third."

More than half the crowd moaned in disgust, ripping up their tickets while the remaining bettors headed to the windows to collect winnings.

"Do over."

The scene whipped around and Mark was once again before the betting window, Kyle beside him.

"You didn't tell me you were going to bet money," Kyle complained.

"Watch and learn, young man," Mark airily replied. When his turn came, he said, "Race one, $1000 exacta, number 5 to win and number 3 to place."

"A thousand dollars," Kyle sputtered. "You crazy?"

"Depends," Mark smoothly replied. "Arrogant Beauty is 4 to 1 odds and Starlight Mist is 3 to 1."

"Where'd you get that kind of money?" he asked, both envious and shocked that Mark would fritter away a grand.

"Been saving for a rainy day. Now be quiet and let's listen to the race."

Like before, as the horses crossed the finish line, the announcer called out, "It's Arrogant Beauty by half a length, followed by Starlight Mist and Dreamweaver in third."

"My God," Kyle burst. "You won."

"That I did," he replied with a nonchalant grin. "Let's see how much I've won."

Kyle's mouth gaped wider as the man behind the wagering window counted out $16,000 in crisp $100 bills and slid them across to Mark.

Stepping aside to readjust the bills to all face the same way, Mark pulled out ten $100 bills and handed them to Kyle. "Here. You can pay me back from your winnings, but you have to follow my lead. OK?"

"O my God," Kyle replied feeling lightheaded.

"Time to bet on the second race. You do exactly as I do."

Mark went back to the window. "Race two, $2 to win on number 7."

Folding the $100 bills and stuffing them in his pocket, Kyle pulled out his wallet and extracted two $1 bills, repeating the same bet.

Back to the TV monitor they went, along with the crowd of bettors to watch the next race. The gates opened and the cheering began.

As the jockeys and thoroughbreds crossed the finish line, the announcer called out, "It's Storm Chaser by a nose, followed by Meadowlark Song and Mystic Mood in third."

"We just lost two dollars," Kyle said with a disappointed frown.

"Not for long. Do over."

Once again the wagering floor and windows swirled in dizzying speed. When the floor and windows settled, Mark and Kyle stood before the wagering window.

"Remember," Mark warned. "Do exactly as I do." Stepping to the window, he placed a thousand dollars on the counter. "Race two, $1000 exacta, number 2 to win and number 7 to place."

Kyle looked down at the cash in his hand then back up at Mark, his face a study in pained resignation.

"Do it," Mark commanded.

"C'mon mister," the man behind the counter urged. "You gonna bet or what?"

With a deep sigh, Kyle placed the same bet. "Easy come, easy go,"

His sadness lasted the duration of the race. By the time the horses crossed the finish line, he was in uncontained euphoric bouncing. "My God," he exclaimed. "You did it again."

"Pretty good odds at 3 to 1 and 5 to 1," Mark grinned.

By the time the eighth race finished, Mark had won close to $150,000 while Kyle pocketed $135,000 after paying back the initial $1,000.

"Can we come back next Saturday?" Kyle begged.

"Let's give it another week or two," Mark cautioned, scrutinizing the surrounding cars in the parking lot. "Did you see the way those guys were looking at us? You have to be less conspicuous. You can't be jumping up and down every time you win and you certainly can't yell out how much you won. No one needs to know how well we're doing."

"My God," Kyle raved, still giddy. "What am I gonna do with all this?"

"Be smart and invest it," Mark advised. "That's what I'm doing."

"I don't know anything about investing. I could use a new truck."

Mark stopped and poked a finger at him. "Do not draw attention to yourself. The last thing we need is the Feds to come here asking us how we got our money and wanting to tax the hell out of it. You got a chunk of change in your pocket. If you're going to spend it all, do it slowly."

Mark was already having buyer's remorse in letting Kyle in on some of the action. He was going to have to be more careful in the future, especially after he moved out into his own place. It wouldn't be long before he had himself a nice mansion, a paid-for nice mansion.

During the next several weeks, Kyle could talk of nothing except horse racing and betting and especially winning. Mark took him once again to the track. By the fourth race, Kyle's exuberance was drawing too much attention and Mark managed to drag his garrulous friend back to the car.

"That's the last time, you hear?" Mark snapped.

"I'm sorry," Kyle protested.

"Sorry's not good enough," Mark shot back. "From now on you're on your own. I'm not helping you anymore."

"C'mon, man," Kyle pleaded. "I'll do better. I promise."

Mark said nothing as he stalked back to the car.

The silence was thick as Mark drove home. Each time Kyle thought to say something, he kept his mouth shut, deciding that he'd let Mark stew for a while. He'd come back around. He always did. Like after the time the girl dressed as Poison Ivy strung him along then dumped him. Mark sulked for a week then was back to normal. This would be the same.

Mark took to avoiding Kyle, especially on weekends. Instead of Cosplay conventions, Mark left Friday evenings for racetracks and casinos out of state, returning late Sunday evenings. By the third weekend, Kyle confronted him outside their apartments.

"I know you're avoiding me," he glared. "Why?"

"You have to ask?" Mark replied. "You know damn well why. Even now, instead of playing it low key, you're still advertising. Look at you. You got yourself a new truck with a lift kit. Folks are sure to be asking how a man who works at a grocery store can afford a truck like that."

"I'll tell 'em it's none of their damn business," Kyle snarled.

"Tell that to the IRS when they come audit you," Mark sharply replied. "And don't even think about implicating me. I'll claim I never knew you."

"What's got into you? We used to be good friends. What happened?"

"You're what's happened."

"You are so full of yourself," Kyle spat. "You think you're the only game in town? Go ahead. I don't need you." He spun around and stormed into his apartment, slamming the door behind him.

"Good," Mark sniffed with relief. "You're a loser anyway."

Two months after receiving the stone, Mark's financial accounts began to blossom, supplemented by bets on horse racing, greyhound racing, card games in casinos, and the stock market. He had moved away from the apartment, purchasing a six-bedroom home in a gated community. Why he still worked as an insurance adjuster was anyone's guess, especially as he now had a personal accountant to handle his financial affairs.

As his wealth accumulated, so did his desire for the nicer things in life. Along with a larger house was a nicer car, better furniture for the larger house, expensive vacations, more expensive cars, a Jacuzzi for the nicer house, and investment opportunities. He reasoned that he could always get more money whenever he needed it.

Yet why did he continue to go to the office? He certainly didn't need the money or the job. Yet each day found him rubbing the stone and saying 'Do over' several times to inflict more verbal abuse on Sheila. There were days where he was truly inspired and heaped scorn and ridicule on her at least a dozen times. There was a consuming and perverse pleasure in demeaning the poor woman who had yet to realize what was happening to her. The pleasure he received from abusing Sheila was worth the hassle of putting up with his coworkers. After all, it was just a matter of time before he told them all to shove it, that he was moving on. But until then, he was having too much fun tormenting Sheila.

But Sheila was not the only object of his attention. There was Derek, a new arrival who seemed to catch Sheila's eye and approval. Derek was a bright-eyed young man, newly married, whose outlook on life was excitement and innocence. This was his first full-time job and he was naively enthusiastic.

For some reason, Derek's effervescent outlook irritated Mark and he thought of ways to put Derek in his place. Sitting in the employee lunchroom one day, Mark carried his tray over to sit with Derek who was seated with a few other new and younger workers.

"Mind if I join you?" Mark said with a winning smile.

"Please," Derek said returning the smile.

"Didn't mean to interrupt the conversation," Mark said, reaching for the salt. "What's the topic?"

"Chad's got girl problems," Derek volunteered, teasing a handsome young man with sculpted face and wavy black hair sitting next to him.

"What seems to be the problem?" Mark asked.

"I can't make up my mind," Chad replied, his confidence bordering in arrogance.

"I know what you mean," Mark nodded. "We all have those problems, don't we Derek."

Derek choked on a forkful of green beans.

"Derek's too devoted to his little wife to let his eyes wander," Chad remarked.

"Oh I don't know about that," Mark snickered. "I've seen the way he leers every time Kathy walks by."

"I do not," Derek objected.

"Now, now, don't be shy," Mark scoffed. "We're among friends here. We're all guys. Isn't that right Chad?"

"She is pretty hot," Chad agreed with a nonchalant grin.

"But I don't –"

"You don't what?" Mark interrupted with a sly grin. "You mean to tell us that you don't think Kathy is attractive?"

"That's not what I said."

"Then you do think she's attractive."

"Well, sure, but –"

"No 'buts' about it," Mark said, turning to Chad. "See? Even Derek thinks she's hot."

"But not like that," Derek complained.

"Don't worry," Mark consoled. "We won't tell the little lady that you're infatuated with Kathy."

"I am not," Derek retorted, a little too loudly so that those in nearby tables paused to pay attention to the commotion.

Mark cast a knowing glance at the surrounding lunch crowd. "He's having problems at home."

"No I'm not," Derek snapped and jerked up to standing.

Mark smiled at him and rubbed the stone. "Do over."

The room whirled and Derek once again choked on a forkful of green beans.

"Derek's too devoted to his little wife to let his eyes wander," Chad remarked.

"Oh," Mark replied, acting surprised. "Say Derek, got any nude pictures of your wife?"

"No," he indignantly replied.

"Want some?" Mark shot back, causing Chad to burst a laugh.

Derek's eyes widened in anger and he thrust his chair back.

"Do over."

For the third time, the room whirled and Derek choked on his forkful of green beans.

"Derek's too devoted to his little wife to let his eyes wander," Chad remarked.

"Really?" Mark commented then turned to Derek. "Where does she work?"

"She works as an administrative assistant for a marketing company," Derek answered.

"Ah," Mark commented then leaned over to Chad, whispering loudly enough for Derek to head. "I hear she's having several affairs at the same time and they all seem OK with it."

"That's a lie," Derek shouted, jumping up.

"Everybody knows what a tramp she is," Mark sneered then, bored with the game, rubbed the stone. "Do over."

This time the room whirled and he was again carrying is tray over to sit with Derek and Chad.

"Mind if I join you?"

Instead of Derek's usual cheerful demeanor, he seemed preoccupied, offering a noncommittal "Sure."

"You OK?" Mark asked.

"Huh? Oh, yeah, yeah. I'm fine," he replied, his smiled forced.

Mark inwardly grinned and debated whether to continue haranguing Derek. Deciding Derek had had enough for today, he settled into a relaxed meal, vowing to continue the game with tomorrow's lunch.

Chapter 2

It was the next morning while he was shaving that he noticed it – grey hair amongst the dark brown. Grabbing a small handheld mirror from the cabinet below the sink, he positioned and tilted the mirror as he gazed at the reflection in the mirror above the sink. His concern morphed to shock when he saw the beginnings of a bald spot at the back of his head. In dismay, he reached up and gingerly probed the bare flesh amidst the thinning hair. Was it possible he was going prematurely grey? But what about the bald spot? His father didn't have a bald spot until he was in his mid-sixties. And the grey...

Mark stepped back to study his face. Aside from the usual morning sleepiness, he looked like he always did. Yet... He leaned closer to examine the once smooth flesh that now seemed to have a wrinkle here and there, especially around the eyes and corners of his lips.

He was just tired, he rationalized. It had to be this damned weather. It rained too much here. He needed a vacation to someplace where the sun shone brightly for most of the year, some place not too hot, but sunny.

Arizona came to mind and just as quickly he castigated himself. Old people go to Arizona for their health and he wasn't old. He wasn't even thirty yet.

But the closer he looked, he swore his skin had the tired look of age. Maybe he was sick, fighting a bug. Those idiots at the office were always coming to work regardless of how sick they were. In fact, Peggy, three cubicles down from him, probably had the flu. The flushed skin, the red watery eyes, and the dry cough didn't stop her from dragging her sorry ass into work out of fear of the wrath of Sheila. Maybe he ought to pay the doctor a visit and get something preventative so he wouldn't catch Peggy's crud.

Pushing aside his disquiet, Mark finished shaving, dressed and headed to the office, rehearsing his latest insults so that he might start the day afresh with a series of mind-numbing insults that were sure to have Sheila cowering in despair.

One area in his life that had also taken a nice improvement was dating. Mark wasn't exactly the broad-shouldered handsome man like Chad. It wasn't that he was unattractive. After all, he exercised regularly and watched what he ate. He was reasonably good-looking, but not the sort of good-looking that women would take a second glance at, especially if there was someone better looking close by, which seemed to occur most of the time.

The appellation most often applied to him was 'rugged.' He had that outdoors quality that some women found attractive. Unfortunately, he hadn't found many women who found that quality desirable.

That changed with his newfound wealth.

He discovered that a sufficient amount of cash would fetch him some of the most attractive women he'd ever seen. Along with hot tub parties and long satisfying sessions in the bedroom, he'd taken to smoking a pipe and wearing a silk bathrobe. Several ladies said he had the looks and joie de vivre of Hugh Hefner. Initially the comparison pleased him until he realized they meant an older Hugh Hefner.

It was the final time in the hot tub with three lovely ladies provided by an escort service that the one brunette, a stunning long legged voluptuous woman, had commented that he looked to be the younger version of the famed hedonist, when he was in his 50s. Shocked at the comparison, his first urge was to chase everyone out. Instead, he enjoyed their company and services then patiently waited until the last one was paid and departed that he vowed no more.

Climbing the stairs to his bedroom, he stared at his reflection in the mirror and was stunned to see that they were closer to the truth than he wanted to admit. Standing before him was an older man, far older than his biological thirty years.

What was happening? Was his fast and loose lifestyle causing him to age? How could that be? Hugh Hefner had packed in a lot more into his first thirty years and looked a lot younger than Mark did now.

There and then, Mark vowed to live a healthier life, eating better and exercising. Yet daytime would find him driving to the office where he would start the morning with the latest invective hurled at Sheila, though occasionally sometimes Derek or one of his coworkers would be on the receiving end.

One morning, Mark noticed the change in Derek. He had circles under his bloodshot eyes and he dragged his feet whenever he walked. Instead of asking Derek about this alteration to his usual chipper demeanor, he asked others, always making sure Derek was close by to know they were talking about him. Gossip was always more fun when the victim knew it was directed at him.

What Mark learned was that Derek's home life was dissembling. The once madly-in-love husband and wife were openly antagonistic to the point that the wife had threatened moving out to a place of her own.

Mark grinned with smug satisfaction. Derek deserved to be brought down for being such a naïve and sappy coworker. Besides, Derek's home life was affecting his work performance and he had fallen out of favored employee status with Sheila.

At the same time, Mark noticed Sheila was beginning to physically change. Her once plump figure had shed so much weight that he was surprised that she actually looked good, especially as she normally dressed quite well. Yet her face was pale and dark, and she had developed a cough.

Standing inside her office, Mark sympathetically chided, "You really ought to be home in bed, you need to take better care of yourself, you fat cow."

"What?" Sheila recoiled with a hacking cough.

"Do over."

Sheila looked up at him, her eyes filmy.

"You really ought to take a few days off to get better," he urged, "you snot-nosed, porcine whore." He liked the word 'porcine', a recent addition to his vocabulary.

Instead of responding, Sheila's jaw slacked open in shock and she bent over in a spasm of coughing.

"Do over."

As Sheila wiped her mouth, Mark offered her his best 'caring' face. "Why don't you go home? I can run things for the few days you need to get better. You can call me to check on things if it will make you feel better."

With a reluctant nod, Sheila resigned herself to missing work for the first time in her almost twenty years of employment there.

"Go on," he encouraged. "You'll get better in no time."

Picking up her purse, she shuffled to the door. With sad dejection, she paused to look out over the cubicles of her domain, adding a long-suffering sigh as she plodded to the door and down the hallway.

Mark abruptly realized he wouldn't have her here to abuse if she was home recuperating. His brief dilemma dissolved as he reminded himself, that's what phones were for.

On the first day of her home recovery, Mark called. "Is this Sheila?"

"Yes," the hoarse voice answered.

"This is Mark, you malignant pus-filled wart of a human being."

"W... what?"

Sheila's coughing caused Mark to pull the earpiece away from his ear.

"Do over. Is this Sheila?"

"Yes," she answered, her voice weaker.

"This is Mark, you putrid pile of porcine excrement." He was pleased he got to use 'porcine' again.

Sheila uttered a low moan of anguished pain and Mark could hear her labored breathing.

"Do over. Is this Sheila?"

There was a pause then a barely audible, "Yes."

"Feeling any better?"

There was a hesitation followed by, "No," as though the response took great effort.

"Well hang in there," he cheerfully replied. "You'll be back in no time."

As soon as he disconnected, he called out, "Derek. Get you sorry ass in here."

With a not-so-subtle glare of defiance, Derek entered Sheila's office, now commandeered by Mark.

"You can't talk to me like that," he said, folding his arms.

"I can talk to you any way I damn well please, you sorry sack of malodorous cow pies."

"What?"

"Do over."

"You can't talk to me like that."

"Yes I can, you putrid pustule of cancerous slime."

Derek's mouth gaped open in shock. "But... but, you can't talk to me like that."

"Do over."

For the next five minutes, Mark belittled and shamed Derek, noting that with each exchange, Derek's posture curled in on itself until by the end of the harangue, Derek looked like a cringing puppy.

"And one last thing. Tell your wife to quit calling me. I don't go out with married women. Now get back to work."

Derek's stunned look was more than satisfying as the beaten employee crawled back to his desk.

Mark sat on the patient's table in the examination room, his mouth slacked open. "What?"

"I said you're in good shape for a fifty-year-old," the doctor commented with a frown as he flipped the charts on the computer monitor.

"But I'm only thirty," Mark objected.

The doctor rubbed his cheek while the frown remained. "That's what's puzzling me. You're fine," he quickly added, seeing Mark's look of gloom. "There's nothing wrong with you. Your cholesterol is a bit high, but a simple change in your diet can fix that. It's just that your other tests suggest someone in his early fifties. It could be a fluke, so let's not get carried away. Let's take a look at you again in six months."

A dejected Mark shuffled out to the counter, paid his bill to an attractive blond who appeared to be in her early thirties, but kept addressing him as "Sir" with a tone that one used with a grandparent.

Vowing to halt the advance of age, Mark returned home and ordered his cook to make only healthy meals. He then joined a fitness club and threw himself into a disciplined regimen that saw him at the club every day.

Yet each workday following would find Mark back in the office reveling in the phone calls to Sheila and the public embarrassment of Derek. Derek's humiliation was particularly enjoyable as Mark shifted to loudly excoriating Derek's wife and her penchant for ignoring her husband and flaunting her affairs.

"Why do you put up with her behavior?" Mark argued one day, Derek standing before the desk, wringing his hands. "I'd have divorced her sorry ass a long time ago."

"But it's not true," Derek meekly replied, less convinced with each passing day.

"Not true?" Mark scoffed. "The last time she was here, she exposed herself right here in this office. You had gone to the break room to get her some coffee. You were barely out the door when she ripped open her blouse, demanding I take her right then. I implored her to behave and, thankfully, she pulled herself together and acted like nothing had happened when you came back. She'll deny it of course if you ask her."

"That's a lie," Derek whined, clutching his chest. "I don't believe it."

"Of course you don't. She's the consummate liar."

"But... but..."

"Do over."

The room spun and once again Derek stood before the desk.

"Your wife called me to tell me she's divorcing you. Said you were pitiful in bed and she's tired of having to satisfy herself with all those other men."

"No," Derek blurted, backing up.

"She also said she'd be happier if you were dead. It would make it a lot easier for her to move on without a nasty divorce."

Derek back-peddled until he bumped into the closed door.

"She also said something about divorcing *you* first, if you didn't have the balls to do it first. Those were her words exactly. When I asked her what she meant, all she said was 'Hitman.' I'd watch my back if I were you."

Derek flung the door open and fled past Janice, a painfully slender woman with short hair that advertised her pinched face.

"What's with him?" she said walking into the office.

"Marital problems," Mark replied, rolling his eyes. "Came in here to complain. Told him to leave his personal life at home."

"Yeah," she nodded. "I heard she's sleeping around on him."

"I heard the same thing."

"You know he's taking meds for depression."

"Really?" Mark brightened.

"Yeah. Don't know if they're doing any good. He's always so down. He used to be such a cheerful guy."

"Well," Mark shrugged. "We all have our problems. What do you need?"

"You wanted to go over the report for Triple A labs." She held up a thick folder.

"I've thought about that. You know what you're doing. Go ahead and take care of it. Just let me know the results."

Surprised and pleased, Janice gave him a thumbs up and strode back to her desk while Mark plotted Derek's demise.

When Monday came around, Mark was pleased to learn that Sheila was in the hospital. Placing Janice temporarily in charge of the office, he went to see his boss.

Much to his disappointment, he was not allowed into the room as he was not related. But he did manage to discover that she had a heart condition and was in critical care. Offering his concern for her health, he arrived back at the office in time to see the squad of police cars outside the building.

Standing just beyond the 'Do Not Cross" yellow tape, he looked up to see a man standing on the ledge outside the fifth story window. With a wicked smile, he recognized Derek. Derek was pressed against the building, palms flat upon the brick, his head dipping forward to take in the growing crowd below.

Mark noticed Derek's wife, Beth, standing just inside the tape, arms folded staring up at her husband. She seemed more irritated than distraught. He also noted that she was very attractive and wondered how long he ought to let her grieve before asking her out.

As the crowd grew, Mark started a low chant.

"Jump. Jump. Jump."

The chant caught on and voices united in the demand. Mark noted that even Beth was caught up in the chant, her lips and voice moving in unison with the others.

Despite the best efforts of the police, the chant grew in volume until it abruptly stopped as Derek did a perfect swan dive off the ledge, crashing headfirst into the concrete walkway, leaving a mangled and grotesque mess. The spectacle over, the crowd dissipated, thrilled to have witnessed the suicide.

Mark walked over and touched Beth on her arm. She startled and looked at him with strangely distant eyes, as though not yet aware her husband was dead.

"Are you OK?" he gently asked.

"I'm fine," she replied without emotion.

"If there's anything I can do, please don't hesitate to ask."

"I'm fine, but thank you."

A policeman came up and escorted her away.

Mark slid a glance back at the contorted wreckage that used to be Derek and grinned. Today was a good day so far.

Sheila's funeral was on the following Sunday. Mark attended the ceremony and was surprised at how few people showed up. Other than sending flowers from the corporate headquarters, no one else from the office was there. One person he noticed was an attractive brunette who turned out to be her sister, Rachel.

"I'm sorry for your loss," he offered, using his best sincere face.

"Thank you. And you are?"

"My name is Mark. I worked with your sister."

"Yes. I remember," she replied. "She said she had promoted a man in her office to be her deputy. That took me by surprise as she rarely ever complimented anyone." She looked around at the few others talking amongst themselves. "I'm surprised you're the only one here from her office."

"I won't make excuses for the others, but some people don't like funerals. Hopefully they've expressed their sympathies via flowers or cards or something else."

The more Mark talked with her, the more he noted the wide gulf in the sisters' personalities. Sheila was an assertive, demanding and acerbic boss. Rachel was a soft-spoken artist and animator. By the time the last person left, Mark had Rachel's phone number.

Mark's attentions to both Rachel and Beth were rewarded with their returned interest, though Beth took a little longer to convince. While neither Rachel nor Beth knew of each other, they were both impressed with Mark's house and lifestyle.

"How can you afford to live in such a grand home on what you make?" Beth asked, awed by the size of the beautifully apportioned home.

"I invest and have been quite successful in day trading on the stock market," he answered, gallantly escorting her around the home. "And besides, I no longer work there. I realized I could make far more on my own than working for someone else."

"You must be very good at it."

"I've been blessed," he replied with a saintly air.

Dinner was an intimate affair on the veranda followed by a visit to Mark's bedroom upstairs. He lounged in the chair by the fireplace, watching Beth undress in a slow seductive rhythm. He held the stone in his hand.

She approached and dropped to her knees and unbuckled his belt. Yanking his trousers down, she devoted her attention to pleasuring him. When the ecstasy exploded, he caught his breath and rubbed the stone.

"Do over."

The scenario repeated another six times until Mark decided it was time to give her return attention. Immediately after each time of her frenzied climax, he rubbed the stone.

"Do over."

After the seventh time, they drifted off to exhausted sleep.

Mark was the first to awaken.

Quietly slipping out of bed, he dressed in silk pajama pants and robe, setting out a robe for Beth before heading downstairs to the kitchen.

"Good morning, Sir," the cook cheerily greeted him.

"Good morning, Nan. Coffee ready?"

"Yes, Sir.   What would Sir like for breakfast this morning?"

"How about some of your world-famous biscuits, scrambled egg whites and chicken sausage."

"Yes Sir."

"I have a guest this morning," he said with an amused smile.

"Very good Sir. I'll make more than enough for two. Where would Sir like his breakfast?"

"On the veranda. Thank you, Nan."

Coffee mug in hand, Mark was midway through the foyer to the living room when he saw Beth descending the stairs. She was barefoot, dressed in the robe.

"Good morning, gorgeous," he suavely said. "Sleep well?"

"Very well, thank you." She sidled up to him, slipping an arm through his and whispered, "You are a god in the bedroom, a stallion."

"Then you are a goddess," he replied, "for you are an exquisite lover."

"I love the way you talk," she complimented then nodded at the mug in his hand. "Any more of that?"

"Of course. Follow me." Taking her hand, he led the way to the veranda where Nan had placed a pot of coffee, creamers, sweeteners and another mug. Pouring her coffee he scooted a chair out for her to sit.

"Thank you." Stirring a thick heavy cream into her coffee, she glanced around at the grounds. "You have a lovely place."

"Thank you."

"Do you miss it?"

"Miss what?"

"Working in an office."

"Not in the slightest. However, the one advantage was that I met you."

"That was nice. I bet you meet lots of women in your affairs."

"None as beautiful as you."

"You are so sweet. You're so different from my former husband. You are so educated and refined. He was such a commoner. I realize that now. At the time, I was too naïve to see it."

Placing a gentle hand on hers, he said, "We all make mistakes at times. Fortunately for you, you were able to move on. That takes a strong person. I'm very impressed."

"Don't be," she said, flipping a hand at him. "Once I realized he was a loser, I was happy to be away from him."

"Speaking of other people," he coyly said. "You are a strikingly beautiful woman. It must be problematic to have to fend off all those suitors, even when you were married."

"There were some," she stated, "but I was true to my marriage, despite the opportunities."

"I wouldn't have blamed you if you had strayed, but again, I'm impressed. Most people I've encountered would have taken advantage of opportunities the moment things became difficult. But then, that's not who you are."

Nan brought out breakfast, placing china plates in front of them then arranging silverware beside the plates.

"Thank you, Nan. This looks delicious as usual."

"This smells yummy," Beth said, inhaling the aromas.

"Nan is the world's best cook," Mark complimented, smiling at his cook.

Nan flushed with pride. "Thank you Sir."

Once the cook returned to the kitchen, Beth serenely smiled, leaning back in the chair, her hands wrapped around the coffee mug. "This is wonderful." Taking a sip, she said, "I was thinking. Why don't I do something for you next weekend?"

"I can't next weekend," Mark said with overt disappointment. Next weekend was Rachel's. "I'll be out of town on business all week and won't be back until late Sunday night. How about the weekend after? And isn't it someone's birthday that weekend?" He gave her his best warm knowing smile.

"Yes," she said, returning his smile.

"Then it's my choice to treat you to something special."

"Like what?"

"Now, now," he replied, waving away her inquisitiveness. "It won't be a surprise if I tell you. But," he said, leaning closer and lowering his voice, "pack a suitcase with clothing for the beach."

Beth's eyes burst wide with pleasure.

"Can you take a few extra days off?"

"Yes."

"How about a week? We leave Friday night and come back the following Sunday. You'd miss five days of work."

"That would be wonderful. Where're we going?"

"Nice try," Marked laughed. "It's supposed to be a surprise."

Despite her continued efforts, Mark rebuffed all her inquiries because, in truth, he had no idea where they were going.

As Beth's 30th birthday approached, Mark decided to find a suitable gift. Yet the perfect gift eluded him until he passed by a jewelry and watch store and his eyes lit upon a ladies Rolex watch in the window. Pausing, he quietly read the card below the watch.

"Pearlmaster, eighteen carat gold with twelve diamond hour markers. $36,500. On sale for $29,999."

With a sly smile, he pushed open the door to the store.

"Good day, sir," an older man standing in front of a tall display case greeted him. "Are we interested in a watch today? A gift perhaps?"

"You are very perceptive," Mark admitted with a grin. "I'm looking for a lady's watch and the one you have on sale in the window, the Pearlmaster for twenty-nine, nine ninety-nine, looks interesting."

"Ah," the man's face lit up. "An excellent choice."

He glided to the display window and delicately removed the watch, returning to present it to Mark to examine.

As Mark lifted the watch to the light, his hand went into his pocket.

"Do over."

In a flash and whirr, he was back home standing in front of the mirror in his bedroom, the watch in his hand. With a loud guffaw, he crossed the room and slipped the watch into the nightstand by the bed.

Half an hour later, he was standing in front of the same jewelry store, the Pearlmaster empty except for the ad card. His eyes lit upon the watch to the left, a ladies Rolex President for $30,000. Suppressing a wide grin, he pushed the door open.

"Good day, sir," the older man, again standing in front of a tall display case greeted him. "Are we interested in a watch today? A gift perhaps?"

"Yes. I'm interested in the ladies Rolex President in the window for 30 K. I'm also interested in loose diamonds."

"Ah," the man's face once again lit up. "Have a seat there," he pointed to a small table, "and I'll be right with you. Are there particular size diamonds you are interested in?"

"Nothing smaller than a carat. Actually, a bit larger would be better, say three carats or larger. Clarity, nothing less than VVS1. And of course, colorless."

"Of course. I see you know your diamonds," the man replied with a respectful nod.

The man startled when he went to retrieve the Rolex. Mark watched him pause and frown as he checked and rechecked the window display case, searching for the missing Rolex Pearlmaster.

"Is there a problem?" Mark asked.

"No, no, no problem," he replied, the worry in his voice obvious.

Mark clamped his mouth shut to keep from laughing at the man's obvious stress.

Retrieving the watch, the man went behind the display counters and opened a safe, withdrawing a metal box. Closing the safe, he quickly glided to the table, sitting opposite Mark.

"Here is the watch," he said, handing the Rolex to Mark.

Mark gave it a cursory glance then set it to the side.

Noticing the greater interest in the diamonds, the man opened the box which had several moveable shelves layered in black velvet, divided in sections large enough to hold an individual diamond in each section. Using a stylus, he pointed to the top shelf.

"These are all a bit over three carats," he explained.

"Do you have anything larger?"

"We have diamonds all the way up to almost nine carats," he proudly replied.

"Then let's look at your largest diamonds," Mark said.

The man gave Mark a quick once-over, paying particular attention to the clothes, recognizing the expense in the wardrobe. "As you wish."

Placing the diamonds back in the box, he returned them to the safe and withdrew another smaller metal box. Coming back to the table, he opened the box.

"This top shelf here," he said, pointing with the stylus, "are all five carats or better. Starting prices around $300,000."

"What about that one?" Mark pointed to the largest diamond.

The man bent over to look at the desired diamond. "That one is 8.29 carats, D color, and VVS1 clarity. The asking price is one million."

Mark's brow furrowed in as though he was deep in thought. "And the ones next to it?"

"Those begin at the low nine hundreds."

Silence settled for only a moment before Mark said, "I'll take the largest four that you have plus the Rolex."

"P... pardon?" the man sputtered.

"I said I'll take the largest four plus the Rolex," Mark answered, arching an eyebrow. "Is there a problem with that?"

"My goodness, no," the man gushed. Picking up the box and watch, he moved to the other side of the counter, selecting a watch box and four small individual diamond boxes. As he placed the watch and diamonds in their respective boxes, he asked, "Do you wish insurance for these?"

"I have my own insurance, thank you" Mark assured him, stepping up to the counter.

The man dipped his head and placed the watch and diamond boxes in a small tote bag. Using the computer monitor's touch screen, the man tallied up the total.

"That will be four million, sixty-nine thousand, three hundred and forty dollars, which includes the tax."

Pinching the top of the bag with thumb and forefinger, Mark pretended to reach for his wallet, instead finding the stone.

"Do over."

The room flashed and whirled and once again. Mark was back home, this time standing outside beside the car. Between thumb and forefinger dangled the bag holding watch and diamonds.

Barking a laugh, Mark went back inside and secured the watch and diamonds in the safe in his study. Wondering if he could rob the store of its complete inventory, Mark drove back to the city and parked his car in the valet parking garage then headed to the store.

By the time Mark finished plundering the store, he had used the stone four more times, increasing the amount of diamonds and precious stones desired with each visit. One thing he couldn't help notice was the man's exponentially increasing agitation each time the missing watches and diamonds were discovered. By the fifth time, the man was in such a nervous condition that Mark decided to plunder another jewelry store.

It was as he was passing an alley that he was pushed from behind and forced into the passageway between two businesses, hustled along by two pairs of strong hands that compelled him forward until he was positioned behind a dumpster and roughly turned around to face his captors.

They were two young men, heavily tattooed on face and arms. One had a lip piercing.

"Give us what you got," one of them threatened, a gun in his hand. He was wiry with short red hair.

"Sure," Mark replied, catching his breath. "You can have it all." He reached into his pocket for the stone.

"Do over."

The alleyway dissolved and spun and he was again outside at home beside the car. Angry that he had almost been assaulted, he went inside to the gun safe, pulling out a 9mm Glock with a short suppressor, three loaded magazines and a shoulder holster. Ensuring his overcoat hid the weapon, he returned to the city. Parking his car, he headed to the jewelry store, this time on the opposite side of the street.

He saw them as they stood outside a pawn shop. Crossing the street, he approached the red head.

"I think you may be able to help me."

The red head gave him a curious look then shot a glance at his partner. "Sure mister. What's on your mind?"

Mark pulled up the sleeve on his overcoat just enough to show his watch. "I've got a watch I need to get rid of. You look like someone who might know someone who could help me. Yes, it's a Rolex."

"What's to stop us from just takin' it?" the red head sneered.

"That would be bad business," Mark replied, giving him a look that declared the man was an idiot. "I've access to more of these. Why would you steal this from me and ruin future business deals?" He turned to the other man. "You interested?"

"Yeah, sure. C'mon into my office." He led the way to the alley then down the passageway. As they approached the dumpster, Mark withdrew the Glock and shot the man with the lip piercing in the back of his head.

Hearing the ping and seeing his partner crumble to the street, red head spun around in time to see the pistol pointed at his head.

"What the he –" was all he got out before Mark fired, drilling him through the forehead.

Holstering the weapon, Mark briefly stared down at the two thugs, adjusted his overcoat and passed on through to where the alley entered onto another main thoroughfare. He felt good as he walked, reliving the scene. Squeezing the trigger and killing both men had given him a satisfaction and pleasure he had not experienced before. They deserved to die, especially after they had threatened him.

He wondered how he might again experience the pleasure of killing some deserving thug. Then the thought emerged that he could simply patrol the streets at night and find suitable suspects, one hand on the stone for any emergency.

His first opportunity came two nights later when he witnessed a teenager knock out an older woman sitting on a park bench. The punch was out of nowhere and the woman collapsed to the ground as the teenager roared in laughter to his two friends. Mark followed them in the distance for a few minutes until they came to a quieter part of the park when he hurried to close the distance between them.

The attacker heard him coming and turned in time to see the companion to his right slump to the ground followed by the second companion to his left. The teenager's eyes burst wide in fright and he had no time to beg for mercy when Mark fired.

Looking quickly around, Mark was relieved that he was alone. Stepping over the sprawled bodies, he made his way to the edge of the park to where the streetlamps gave shadowed light to the surrounding sidewalks and closed businesses. Cabs and autos, their low beams illuminating the tar-patched road in front, passed by, their occupants impervious to the dead bodies not more than one hundred feet away.

Mark hitched up the collar of his overcoat and strolled the sidewalk around the park, back to the bench where the older woman had regained her wobbly consciousness. His first inclination was to see if she was OK. But as he glanced around to see if anyone was close by to assist, he saw that they were quite alone.

A sudden perverse emotion pulsed though him and before he had a chance to analyze it, the gun came out just as her pathetic and frightened eyes caught his, and he fired, watching her body jerk back at the impact then slump over onto the bench.

Shouldering the pistol, Mark strode away, his mind awhirl at the aftermath when the police discovered or were notified that a woman and three teenagers were dead in the park. He imagined the conundrum they would face as they tried to piece together the connection between the woman and the teenagers.

With a grin and a shrug, he headed to his car.

The week with Beth went almost as planned. They flew to Bermuda and spent the days on the beach, riding horses, wind surfing, snorkeling, and sightseeing. Evenings were at the finest restaurants followed by love-making sessions back in the hotel suite with Mark using the stone when it was her time to pleasure him for he had discovered that his anticipation and excitement seemed to increase with each successive do over until about the eighth time when his strength sluffed away so much that he nearly fell asleep.

Yet there was one thing that he couldn't help but observe and that was the way Beth cast sly glances at the younger men, those closer to her age. They were both startled one evening when a curious patron commented that it was so nice to see a father and daughter sharing a vacation.

Mark's indignation burst and he snapped, "She's my fiancée."

The woman's face said it all, the look of bemused condescension followed by the knowing wink.

Mark's sour disposition consumed him until Beth said, "Ignore her. She's just jealous."

"That's very sweet of you," he answered, relaxing only a little.

"Did you mean it?"

"Mean what?"

"Fiancée."

"I was going to surprise you tonight," he sighed with a doleful look. "But now that my secret is revealed, shall I await your answer until I can properly pose the all-consuming question?"

"I can give you my answer now," she replied, her face flushed with happiness. "Yes."

Mark's mouth split into a wide grin. "I will make you the happiest woman on the earth," he firmly intoned. Yet his mind raced because he had no intention of marrying her or anyone else for that matter. Why he said 'fiancée' puzzled him though it was the first thing that came to mind. Marrying her would certainly put a damper on his relationship with Rachel, and between the two, he preferred Rachel. And he certainly wasn't going to marry Rachel.

Still, there was no need to ruin the week by admitting the truth. He would let Beth delight in the thought of marriage and break it off after a suitable time. A sudden amusing thought surfaced. He would build up the marriage motif, maybe to the point of sending out invitations then call it off or perhaps have Beth catch him in a compromising position, but not with Rachel. He was still enjoying her. It would require some thought and planning, but done right, it would destroy Beth.

Staring across the table at the very attractive woman, he suddenly felt bored with her. She was superb in bed, but she lacked intellectual depth. Likewise, he doubted she would be so accommodating with his occasional desire for multiple bed partners at the same time. The thought of being married, let alone being faithful, to one woman gave him a sudden tremor of apprehension.

"Are you OK?" Beth asked.

"Of course. I was just thinking of all the planning that needs to happen."

As soon as he said it, ennui filled him. He had accomplished what he had set out to do: get rid of Derek and sleep with his wife. Why did he need to prolong the inevitable? Still, he didn't want to ruin the time here in Bermuda. He would wait until they returned then simply cut off all contact with her.

Yet the patron's comment crept back into his thoughts. "Why did she think I was your father?" Beth's awkward stare caused him to frown. "Do I look that much older?"

"Let's just say that it's hard for someone to look at you and believe that you're only thirty. Don't be offended." She patted his hand. "You look like one of those male models you see in advertisements, the older man who is physically fit and has it all."

Only slightly mollified, Mark smiled as though her words had salved his hurt. Yet he knew the truth; he was aging faster and he didn't understand why. The damned doctors gave him the 'I-don't-know' shrug and explained it away as a case of Werner syndrome. Yet he had none of the associated problems other than what one doctor called Mönckeberg arteriosclerosis, a calcium build-up within the walls of the arteries that usually affected men older than 50.

The thought that his biological clock was ticking faster than everyone else gave him a sense of urgency, a desperation to live life here and now. He had rationalized that many individuals were cut off in the prime of their lives:

hit by a bus, killed in an auto crash, killed by a stray bullet in a gang war, or any of the other innumerable ways to die. That he was still in his prime reminded him that he had to cram the experience of life into every second before he too was taken away by some freak accident.

"You're not here," Beth teased with a sly smile. "I think we need to adjourn to our room where I can show you my appreciation for this lovely meal."

Mark smiled as his hand dropped to feel the stone in his pocket. He would put it to good use again. Perhaps he would last longer than eight times.

When they returned to the room, Mark announced, "I haven't given you your birthday gift yet."

Locking the door, Beth's eyes brightened as she watched him go to the bedroom and return with two small, wrapped boxes.

"The first is your birthday gift." He handed her the smaller of the two boxes.

Unwrapping it, her eyes glowed when she saw the embossed name 'Rolex' on the outside of the box.

"You bought me a Rolex?" Opening the box, she gazed down at the watch then back up to him, her countenance a mixture of joy and wonder. "How... how much did this cost?"

"You're not supposed to ask how much a gift cost," he chided with a smile. "But, if you really want to know, I got it at a steal for only $30,000."

"$30,000?" Beth choked. "Thirty... thousand... dollars?"

"Put it on," he chuckled.

"I'll be afraid to wear this," she said, placing the watch around her left wrist.

"You'll get used to it" he nonchalantly replied. "Now for the pièce de résistance." He handed her the second gift, a small, elongated box, wrapped in simple gold paper.

Tearing off the paper, she opened the box to gape at five large diamonds.

"O my God. These are huge."

"Chose one for your ring and we'll have the rest put into a necklace or ear-rings or something else."

"O my God," she repeated, her eyes brimming with tears.

"I didn't mean to upset you," he teased.

"I love you so much," she gushed, closing the lid. "I'll decide later. Right now, I need to thank you properly."

She placed a finger on his chest and gently pushed him backwards to sit in an overstuffed armchair. As she dropped to her knees he pulled out the stone.

"Why do you always have that stone with you," she asked.

"It's a long story. But the short of it is that it's sort of a talisman."

"Talisman?"

"It means something like a good luck piece," he explained, mildly frustrated that she didn't know the word, "though it's more than that. It was given to me a long time ago by a man who was a father figure to me. I suppose it's more sentimental than anything else, but it means a lot to me and it reminds me that I have so much to be thankful for, like having you."

"That's so sweet," she sighed contently, unbuckling his belt.

Back home, Mark immediately cut off all contact with Beth. It took almost a month before she ceased showing up at the main gate, and a bit longer for the phone calls, voicemails, emails, IM's and letters to stop.

In the beginning, he would dutifully read each bit of correspondence. But as time wore on, he grew bored with her whining and simply deleted messages or trashed letters, especially the weird nude pictures she sent of herself, her mascara running because of the tears she shed. Besides, he had found a new love interest in addition to Rachel.

She was a prim petite woman with large brown eyes who dressed quite conservatively. Her name was Angela and she worked as a receptionist at a hotel in Savannah. Ever patient, Mark took his time with her, his urbane manner finally breaking through her adamantine refusals.

"I normally don't go out with older men," she explained, waiting for him to open the car door for her.

"But I finally wore you down?" he joked.

"Yes," she replied with a fetching smile.

During the dinner that evening, Mark found himself captivated. She had a subtle energy that bespoke someone in control of herself yet willing to taste all that life had to offer. The more time he spent with her, the more he wanted to be with her. So much so that Rachel found herself in the same situation as Beth – forgotten, discarded like yesterday's news.

Suffering through the same ordeal of pleading voicemails, emails and other means of correspondence, Mark seriously considered selling his home and moving to Savannah but reconsidered when he admitted that he still hadn't bedded the lovely Angela. But that was just a matter of time.

In between the visits to Savannah, Mark continued building his portfolio. He had cleaned out most of the jewelry stores in town and had started working the stores in the next city. At night, he continued roaming the streets, his Glock loaded and ready.

The news stories exploded with the rash of murders.

"You're really sweet, you really are," Angela soothed on that fateful evening, placing a hand against his cheek, "but you're too old for me. It's not that I don't care for you. I do. It's just that I can't see much of a life together. I need someone closer to my age, someone I can grow old with. Can you understand that?"

Mark face tightened and he stepped away. "Yes," he spoke, his voice harsh and cold. "I do understand that." Opening the door, he walked out into the night.

But he did not go back to his hotel. Instead, he drove around the block and parked close to her house then waited in the shadows until a car drove up and a man emerged. He was tall and broad shouldered. No sooner had he pressed the doorbell that the door opened and Angela walked out, slipped an arm through his and descended the steps.

That long evening, Mark waited for the car to return. It was close to 1 a.m. when the car skidded to a halt in front of her house. The man got out and opened her door then escorted her to her front door where they embraced and kissed before she invited him in.

The wait wasn't as long as Mark expected, for the man was back in his car less than an hour later. Mark waited until the man drove away before starting his car and following him. Twenty minutes later, it stopped before a two-story townhouse in an upscale neighborhood across the river in South Carolina.

Mark was already out of the car when the man emerged.

"I say, pardon me," Mark said in his most cosmopolitan voice as he walked up. "Might I have a word?"

The man warily regarded him, his hand still on the car's door handle. "What do you want?"

"Nothing serious, I assure you," Mark soothed. "It's just that I couldn't help notice that you were with a friend of mine tonight."

"Yeah? Suppose I was. What's it to you?"

"Well, this is rather embarrassing, but you see, we're married."

"What? She never said she was married," he uttered. "Wait a minute. If you're married, how come you don't live there?"

"We're separated."

"Then it really doesn't matter if you're married or not," he tartly replied, closing the door.

"I suppose not," Mark answered, pulling out the Glock and firing two shots into the man's chest.

Without a word, Mark returned to his car and drove home.

Chapter 3

For the ensuing year, Mark spent more of his time in Savannah, occasionally going home to check on investments and to walk the streets at night. But the time in Savannah was spent spying on Angela.

Four more men were found shot to death in various parts of the city. Two lived in South Carolina. The common link was that they all had dated Angela.

It was late one night as he was tailing the fifth man that he was accosted by a pushy panhandler on East River Street.

"Hey man. You look like you can afford to part with a few bucks."

It was the way he said it, the tone almost a sneer intimating that Mark didn't deserve to have or keep his wealth, that he was obligated to share all of what he had.

Letting his quarry escape unawares, Mark stopped and studied the panhandler. He held a small handwritten sign that read "Homeless, Need Food." Though dressed in worn clothing, Mark noted the man was cleaner than expected of one living on the kindness of strangers.

"Tell you what," Mark smiled. "Let me buy you dinner and then I'll give you all the cash I have on me."

When the man's eyes lit up, Mark noticed the flash of smugness mixed with the triumph of a good night's hustle.

"I know a good Italian place," Mark offered. "You can't go wrong with Italian."

"Plenty of restaurants right here," the panhandler pointed out.

"Too expensive. If you want all my cash, why spend too much on a meal?"

"You can use a credit card."

"I don't have credit cards. I only use cash."

Mark suppressed a grin when he saw the man's overt avarice at the approaching score.

He motioned for the man to accompany him as he headed up River Street Access road. Crossing Bay Street, Mark led him to Johnson Square.

"We'll cut through here," he explained. "It's faster."

The park was deserted at this late hour. As they passed by several benches, Mark dropped back slightly, reached in to pull out his gun from the shoulder holster and placed the silencer barrel against the man's back.

The panhandler noted something hard against his back at the same moment Mark pulled the trigger. Mark fired twice more into the man's back. Catching him as he fell, Mark lugged him onto a nearby bench, arranging the body as though sleeping.

Casting a rapid glance around the park, Mark strode purposely across the paths then over to West Bay Street. By the time the police were notified of a body in Johnson Square, Mark was back at the hotel, in bed, sound asleep.

The next morning, after a leisurely breakfast at Goose Feathers Café and Bakery, Mark decided it was time to return home. Besides, if he continued racking up bodies in Savannah, it was just a matter of time before the police came knocking on his door.

But there was one more thing he needed to do.

That evening, with the top down on his BMW, Mark drove through midtown until he hit East Victory Drive then headed east towards Tybee Island. As he crossed the bridge over the Wilmington River, he flung the pistol over the bridge and into the water.

When he was in South Carolina the following morning, travelling up Interstate 77, he saw the police car behind him, lights flashing. With an irritated sigh, he pulled to the side of the road.

"Is there a problem, Officer?"

While his partner remained in the cruiser running a check on the license plate, the officer came up to the driver's side. He was a trim man with close cropped hair and a no-nonsense smile.

"Where you headed?" the officer asked, studying Mark's driver's license.

"Back home. May I ask why I've been stopped? I wasn't speeding."

The officer peered intently at the license then at Mark and back to the license. "You're 31 years old?"

"I have a rare genetic disorder," Mark lied. "I age a lot faster than normal people."

Frowning, the officer returned to the cruiser, spoke a few minutes with his partner then returned.

"Sorry to have stopped you, Mister Sothby, but we've been notified of a person driving a vehicle fitting your description as a possible link to a series of murders in Savannah."

"You got to be kidding," Mark scoffed.

"Have you been in Savannah recently?"

"Yes. I spent the past several weeks there. I have business connections in Savannah."

"Would you please step out of the car?"

"This is ridiculous," Mark huffed, taking extra effort to pry himself from the car to ensure the policeman noted he was an old man.

"Will you allow us to search your car? You can say 'no', but then we will ask you to follow us back to the station."

"Go ahead." Mark pursed his lips and crossed his arms.

"Please open the trunk."

Mark hit the access button on the remote while the officer's partner emerged. Two minutes later, the partner stood erect, holding the gun case in his hand. Opening it, he extracted a loaded magazine.

"Mark Sothby," the first officer announced, "I'm arresting you on suspicion –"

"Do over."

The scene whirled and an instant later, Mark was outside his hotel, standing beside his car, his luggage on the ground by the trunk.

Silently cursing his stupidity, Mark retrieved his empty gun case with the loaded magazines. Loading the rest of his luggage and securing his car, he carried the gun case to the dumpsters behind the hotel's restaurant.

Satisfied no further evidence of his criminal activity was present, he set off for home only to be stopped at the same spot.

The scene replayed itself to include him standing by the car, his arms folded. After ten minutes of searching, the officers found nothing.

"Sorry to have bothered you, Mister Sothby," the officer said with a hint of disappointment. "You be careful driving home."

As Mark drove off, he pondered who could have outed him. The only person who knew him well enough to describe him and the car was Angela. His first inclination was to turn around and permanently handle the situation.

Instead, he decided that he was pushing his luck. The long nights of surveillance along with a diet of fast food had added weight and he vowed to get back in shape. But it wasn't so easy anymore. His joints and muscles ached on a regular basis and he swore the face staring back at him in the mirror was his grandfather.

Besides, he would return to Savannah, taking pains to be noticed, conduct business and ensure that nothing untoward happened. It would confuse the police.

Yet what aggravated him more than the aches and pains was that people were treating him like an old man. Younger women his age called him 'Darling' or 'Sweetheart.' Despite his best efforts in the gym, he still looked like an old man.

Then he noticed that his reaction speed had slowed considerably. Returning home, he had taken to prowling the streets again. The last time he had gone vigilante, he had been lucky. The two hoodlums he shot were quick and he only winged the second one. It took three more shots to bring him down. He knew then that he would have to give up his evening joy of taking out the human trash.

However, there was a perverse joy in casing the jewelry stores. Here he used his age to his advantage for no one would ever believe an old man could rob a jewelry store.

In addition to using the 'Do over' stone for robbing jewelry stores and winning horse races, Mark took to taunting individuals who irritated him: clerks at check-out counters, salesmen and women at various stores, passersby in the park.

One young lady at the grocery store caught his attention. She wore a name tag that said 'Taffy.' She was a plump girl who seemed more interested in texting than helping shoppers. When asked where a particular item was located, she'd huff in exasperation and point. "Go look in aisle four." Naturally the item in question was never in aisle four.

The first time Mark used the stone on her brought him great satisfaction. She was on aisle 12 stocking soup cans.

"Pardon me you obese porcine slut." He grinned that he got the chance to use 'porcine.'

"What?' The woman leaped to her feet.

He was surprised at her speed.

"Do over."

The aisle whirred and he was again standing before her.

"Excuse me you fat slobbery cow."

"What?"

"Do over."

For the next ten minutes, Mark used all the vitriol he could remember. Each succeeding time, the woman got up slower and slower, until the last time when she had to force herself to stand, clutching her chest.

Mark returned to the store every day after that, specifically seeking her out. By the end of the week, he noticed she was sick with a chest cold. After three weeks, she was in the hospital.

From then on it was only a matter of deciding whom to abuse. The perverse pleasure he received in tormenting and imposing physical ailments on others became his only joy.

His love life also suffered. He couldn't convince young attractive women that he was really only 31 years old. When he tried to explain he had a medical condition, they were either matronly sympathetic or repulsed.

The thought of dating someone his physical age disgusted him. Why should he be forced to settle for some old crone when he was only 31? It wasn't fair. Yes, money still bought companionship, but no young attractive woman wanted a real relationship with him. Oh, there had been the women looking for the Sugar Daddy, but he was too smart for that. Money didn't buy love.

It was late one evening in the early fall when Mark answered the doorbell. He frowned at the grimy man staring expectantly at him. A frayed baseball cap covered stringy hair and a wild beard hid most of his face. He wore a stained Army field jacket buttoned up to his throat. His hands looked like a grease mechanic who hadn't washed in a month.

"How'd you get past the gates?" Mark curled a lip, immediately sensitive to the man's odor.

The man furrowed his brows in concentration as he stared at Mark, studying his face. "I waited for a car to go through and snuck in behind," he answered. "It is you, isn't it? Mark from the Queensbury apartments?"

Mark arched an eyebrow at the mention of his former residence. "Who are you and what do you want?"

"You *are* Mark," the man repeated. "I recognize that voice and tone anywhere. Man, you don't know how long it's taken me to find you. I figured if anyone could help me, you could. Though you look different than I remember. Richer... a lot older."

Mark returned the stare with a cold detached gaze. "Why would I help you?"

"You did once," the man answered.

"I doubt it. I'm not in the habit of giving money to the homeless." He started to close the door when the man jammed a foot in the doorway.

"Mark. It's me. Kyle."

"Kyle," Mark repeated, trying to remember the name when clarity hit. "Kyle? Good God, is that you? What happened?"

"I ran into a stretch of bad luck."

"I haven't seen you in... how long's it been?"

"Almost two years."

"What happened?"

"Like I said, I ran into a stretch of bad luck."

Mark looked past him. "Where's that truck of yours?"

"Repossessed."

"Repossessed? Why?"

"I couldn't make the payments."

"Couldn't make the payments?" Mark gave him a skeptical glance. "You had close to two hundred grand when I left. What happened to that?"

Kyle's voice grew quiet. "I spent it."

"You spent it," Mark repeated, his eyes growing cold. "You spent two hundred grand on what? A place to live? Obviously not because you look like you've been dumpster diving. What did you blow two hundred grand on?"

"Just stuff."

"Just stuff. And now you want me to bail you out again. Is that it?"

"I… if you could see your way clear to loan me a few bucks, to hold me over. Sorta help get me back on my feet."

"What happened to that career you had at the grocery store?"

Kyle's jaw clenched. "They let me go."

"Why? You were a stellar employee."

Instead of answering, Kyle cleared his throat. "May I come in?"

Mark studied him for a moment then in an abrupt change of attitude, opened the door. "I'm sorry. Of course. Have you eaten? I can see what the cook has in the fridge. Why don't you spend the night? You can get cleaned up and I'll send out for some clothes for you."

Kyle's eyes misted and tears formed. "Thank you."

"Nonsense. It's the least I can do for an old friend."

An hour later, Kyle had showered, shaved off the offensive beard and now sat in the grand kitchen, wolfing down a prime rib sandwich and a bottle of Belgian ale. He wore Versace slacks and shirt that Mark had dug out from old clothing he had in a donation bag. Mark sat opposite him, sipping a glass of Screaming Eagle Cabernet Sauvignon.

"You must tell me all that has happened since we last parted," Mark said with his best cultured tone.

"There's not a lot to tell," Kyle said between bites.

"What happened at the grocery store?"

"Aw, they were being asses," he answered, chugging the ale.

"About what?"

63

"Aw, just 'cause I missed a couple days work."

Mark narrowed his gaze at him. "You've never missed work before."

Kyle shrugged. "I sorta got plastered. Woke up two hundred miles away in some cheap ass hotel. Don't remember how I got there, but my money and phone were stolen and I had to hitchhike back home."

Mark peered intently at his former friend. The man looked beat up and used... and common. He marveled that he had once been so close to the man. It was too apparent the cultural gulf between them.

Mark had found the power of words and he had become intoxicated with them, not just in their ability to inflict pain, but also in their ability to confuse and impress. His vocabulary had exponentially expanded and he studied and read to improve his power.

But Kyle? Kyle was and would forever be a low-class rube, a user, a drain on someone's existence. His concept of living was a truck with a lift kit, drinking beer and partying. The man had no culture. And that was the problem. How can one justify a man's existence whose sole quest is to get himself eliminated from the gene pool by doing something stupid while half-intoxicated?

The worst part was that Kyle had found him and Mark knew that once found, he would never be able to get rid of him. That would have to change.

"So the grocery store wouldn't take you back after you explained your situation?"

"Naw. They said it wasn't the first time. Got any more beer?"

"Certainly. Another of the same?" Mark pushed away from the table.

"Uh, this isn't bad. Got any lite beer?"

Mark stared at him waiting for the punchline. Realizing the man was serious merely confirmed his assessment of the man's inferiority. That he would want some cheap watered-down substitute over a quality $15 bottle of excellent Belgian brew spoke volumes.

"Um, no. I don't drink lite beer."

"Then I'll take another of these." He lifted the bottle then looked around the kitchen. "You got a nice setup here. Nice place. How many servants you got?"

"Three," he replied prying open the flip-top to the beer bottle, "a cook, maid, and gardener."

"They live here?"

"No." He placed the bottle by the unused beer glass in front of Kyle.

"You still working at the insurance place?"

"No. I handed in my resignation after Sheila passed away." He watched in morbid fascination as Kyle chugged several gulps of beer, wondering how anyone could taste the excellent brew when it bypassed the tongue.

"I thought you hated her," Kyle replied then belched.

"I never cared for the woman, but she wasn't the reason I left," he lied. Once Sheila died and Derek's marriage and life were destroyed there wasn't any reason to stay. "I needed to focus on my financial portfolio."

"Still doing the horse racing?" Kyle asked, giving him a knowing glance.

Ah, now we come to the real reason for you being here. Mark peered at him over the rim of his wine glass.

65

"Yes, I do. In fact, I've made a substantial income from the horses. I've even managed to buy a few of my own, with partners of course."

"Yup," Kyle nodded. "I knew you'd do good. You had the knack." He set the bottle down and gave Mark an innocent stare. "Maybe you'd see fit to give me another shot."

"We can talk about it. For now, enjoy your meal and get some rest. You look like you could use a good night's sleep. I'll show you around the place in the morning."

It was after lunch by the time Kyle roused himself up from the bed. Slipping the clothes on from the night before, he ambled down the wide staircase, encountering the maid in the foyer who pointed him to the veranda where Mark sat nibbling on pâté and thinly sliced beef tenderloin.

"Sorry I slept so long," Kyle sheepishly said then frowned at the plates of meats, cheeses, bread, rolls, vegetables and deserts. "There's enough food here for ten people," he commented.

"Thought you might be hungry."

"I am," he announced, plopping down to slather a bread roll with mustard to make a sandwich. Layering the bread with meat and cheese, he looked past Mark to the expansive yard. "How big is this place?"

"I have 25 acres, all surrounded by a tall brick wall. We all like our privacy in the neighborhood."

"Neighborhood?" Kyle said, snorting a laugh. "You can't even see your neighbors." His grin widened when he saw the small cooler to the side of the table, filled with lite beer. "Appreciate the kindness." Popping open a can, he downed half, gave a low burp then refocused his attention on devouring the sandwich.

Kyle pointed in the distance to where the gardener was working with a backhoe. "What's he doing?"

"I've decided to plant a tree there. He's preparing the hole for the tree."

"How big a tree you planting?" Kyle frowned. "You could plant a full-grown oak there."

"I intend to."

Kyle turned around and looked up at the third story windows. "How big is the house?"

"A little over 8,000 square feet."

"You could get lost in a place like this."

"It's adequate, for now," Mark replied with a condescending smile.

Kyle returned his smile. "So. You thought about what I said last night, about the horses?"

"Yes, I have and I've decided to give you another chance."

"Hot damn," Kyle exclaimed, slapping his leg.

"There are races tomorrow," Mark explained. "I've a race program that we can look over. Like before, you need to follow my lead and do exactly what I tell you to do. No questions."

Kyle bobbed his head. "No problem. I'll do just like before."

That evening, Mark and Kyle sat at a table in the far part of the estate, next to the hole for the tree. On the table was a bottle of Sauterne with two glasses. On the ground beside Kyle's chair was a cooler with ice and lite beer. On a smaller table to Mark's right was a camera and a small mahogany box, a little larger than a cigar box. Behind them was the golf cart that Mark used to travel around his 25 acres.

"Seems an odd place for a talk," Kyle said, popping a can open.

"You sure you don't want to try the Sauterne? It's quite good. It's a Chateau D'Yquem."

"Naw. Looks too fancy to me. Besides, I'm just a county boy who likes his beer." He swigged down half the can. "So, what're we talking about out here?"

"The future, my friend," Mark replied, holding his glass up in toast.

"Hear, hear," Kyle grinned, holding up the beer can.

"Yes, the future," Mark continued. "There is money to be made in the future. It's ours for the taking."

"Damn straight," Kyle cheered, downing the rest of the beer then popping open another.

"Here now," Mark said. "I brought the camera. We need to record this moment."

"Why not just use your phone?"

"How plebian," Mark sniffed. "While phone cameras certainly are good, they can't compete with a Nikon."

"Whatever," Kyle said with a belch.

Mark stood and retrieved the camera. "Stand by the edge so I can get a picture."

"Don't you think it's getting too dark?"

"Low lighting is what makes the picture," Mark explained. "That's why I use the Nikon."

Kyle stood up, a little wobbly, and half-staggered over to the edge of the hole to peer down. "It's deeper than I thought... and big."

"Turn around."

Obeying, Kyle turned, casting a wary glance at the cavity behind him.

"Look at me. Now hold your beer can up. That's it."

There was a flash causing Kyle to blink in blindness. "Can't see a thing."

"You closed your eyes. Let me take another. Keep your eyes open this time. Look into the camera."

The flash added to Kyle's blindness.

"OK, just one more. Hold on a second." Kyle opened the box and withdrew a pistol with a silencer attached. "OK. Give me that pose again."

Still blinking, Kyle raised the beer can up and gave Mark a loopy smile. He heard the soft ping at the same time he felt the pain explode in his chest followed by the sensation of falling. Then darkness swallowed up his soul.

Mark walked over to the edge and peered down to where Kyle lay sprawled on his back, the beer can still in his hand, the widening blood pool staining his shirt.

"Never really cared for that shirt," Mark said with a shrug then pumped three more rounds into Kyle's chest.

Walking back to the table, he placed the gun back in the box then jammed a hand in his pocket to rub the stone.

"Do over."

The yard whirled and he stood at the edge of the hole looking down at Mark's body.

Frowning, he rubbed the stone again.

"Do over."

The scene repeated and he again found himself at the edge of the hole.

By the third time, Mark knew the act was not reversible. He reasoned that the stone could not undo death. While the thought dissatisfied him at some levels, he relished the idea that he had killed someone he knew without so much as a blink of an eye. Yes, he recognized that he was responsible for Sheila's death and Derek's suicide, but Sheila's death had taken too long and Derek's had been by his own hand. With Kyle, it had been well planned, efficient, and easy, too easy.

Starting the backhoe, he maneuvered the machine and scooped up a bucket load of dirt and dumped it into the hole. He continued until the hole was filled then ran the backhoe over the dirt, packing it down before parking it on top.

He then folded the tables and chairs and loaded up the golf cart. Leaning against the cart, he calmly finished his wine before placing the beer and wine bottle on the front seat. Giving one last look at the area, he smiled, pleased with himself, and drove back to the house.

Chapter 4

Mark celebrated his 32nd birthday by staying at home, alone. Shuffling through the foyer to the kitchen to find a snack, he heard the doorbell and diverted his purpose to open the door. Peering through the peephole, he saw that it was cold and drizzling. Two men in suits and rain overcoats stood illuminated by the overhead porch light.

Unlocking and opening the door, he said, "May I help you?"

One man, middle aged though still lean, smiled with only his lips. "Mister Sothby?"

"Yes?""

"I'm Inspector Callahan with the Savannah CID." He flashed a wallet holding a badge. "This is Inspector Nichols." The other man, a head shorter and broader, carrying a cheap briefcase, likewise flashed a badge. "May we come in?"

"Yes, certainly." He opened the door wider, quickly closing it behind them. "It's a nasty day out there."

"Yeah, certainly is," the shorter man replied without emotion as he took in the grandness of the foyer.

"You're a long way from Savannah," Mark commented.

"We're on a case and we'd like to ask you a few questions," Callahan replied. "We understand you spend quite a bit of time in Savannah."

"I have business there," he answered. "Would you like a cup of coffee?"

"Sounds good," Nichols replied with that same emotionless voice.

"Come into the kitchen and we can talk there."

"Nice place you have here," Nichols commented.

"Thank you."   Mark led them into the large kitchen where Nichols pulled out a stool and seated himself at the island, placing the briefcase on the floor, while Callahan stood next to him. Pouring three cups of coffee, Mark placed two cups on the island in front of the visitors.

"Now how can I help you?"   He wrapped his hands around the mug for warmth.

"Where do you usually stay when you are in Savannah?" Callahan asked.

"At the Indigo in the historic district."

Nichols flashed a triumphant glance at Callahan then reached down for his briefcase. In a deliberate display of melodrama, he flicked open latches and withdrew a large mania envelope, handing it to Callahan.

Callahan reached inside and pulled out several photos, placing them on the island table then twisting them around and spreading them out for Mark to see.

Mark tensed when he looked at the first photo. The angle was from higher up but it showed him standing at the trunk of his car, holding the gun case. The succeeding pictures followed him to the dumpster behind the restaurant. The last few photos showed him tossing the case into the dumpster.

"We retrieved these from your gun case," Nichols said, pulling out two loaded magazines tucked securely in evidence bags. "They have your fingerprints on them."

"So?"

"Where's the gun?" Callahan asked.

"What gun?"

Nichols snorted a derisive laugh. "You tossed away a gun case with two good fully loaded magazines. The spot for the gun is empty."

"I don't know what you're talking about," Mark calmly replied. "I found that gun case. Thought about taking it home then changed my mind."

"You found the gun case," Callahan repeated with overt disbelief.

"Yes. I found it in Johnson Square one evening when I was walking home. I picked it up, saw what was inside it, looked around for an owner then decided I might have a need for such protection. Since I don't know much about guns, I'd have to have a gun shop tell me the kind of gun the magazines would fit."

"You expect us to believe that?" Nichols smirked.

"I don't care if you believe me," Mark shrugged. "It's the truth."

Nichols pulled out another large envelope and slid it across the table to him. "Go ahead. Take a look."

Placing his coffee mug down, Mark picked up the envelope and lifted out more photos. This time they showed him with the homeless man. But the pictures weren't clear and it was difficult to make out that it was Mark.

"What are these?" Mark asked, holding one up and pretending to concentrate on the photo, noting the date-time stamp on the lower right corner.

"They're photos of you with a homeless man who was found murdered at that same spot," Nichols said, hiding his frustration that the pictures weren't more damning.

"First," Mark said with dripping disdain, "there is a snowball's chance in hell that I would willingly place myself in the company of a homeless person. Second, I was in my hotel room when this picture was taken. You can check the hotel records."

Mark silently thanked the gods that he always used a timer to start the TV in hotel rooms when he was out doing his business and errands. He liked having the sound on whenever he came back to the rooms, especially as he tended to spend more time alone these days. It was as though someone was there in the room with him and it made him feel less lonely.

"Third, what makes you think that's me?"

"We have an eyewitness," Callahan asserted.

Mark handed the photos back to Nichols. "Your eyewitness is mistaken. I was in my hotel room. You can check the records."

"We did," Callahan replied. "The security cameras show you returning to the hotel not long after these photos were taken."

Mark's mind raced. He had forgotten about the security cameras. "I probably stepped out to get something from the car."

"That's what we thought might have happened," Callahan nodded, "but there's no video of you leaving to check your car. In fact, the only time you left the hotel was earlier that morning."

Mark sipped his coffee, straining to think of some alibi, but nothing crystallized that made any sense. Then a perverse though invaded his anxiety causing him to smile.

"Well, I might as well admit it. Yeah, I killed him. And I killed the others too."

"What others," Nichols brightened, taking out a small handheld recorder.

For the next ten minutes, Mark confessed to all the killings he had committed then confessed to more and more until Nichols finally stopped him with a hard frown.

"You're telling me you killed Kennedy?"

"Yup, that was me on the grassy knoll."

"Damn it all," Nichols snapped. "Stop playing games."

"You got your confession," Mark pointed out. "That's what you wanted. And just think of the fame you'll get when you tell them that you caught Kennedy's killer."

Flicking off the recorder, Nichols sat back in a huff. "You're wasting our time."

Mark grinned at him. "Do over."

The kitchen spun around in dizzying speed and Mark found himself standing in the living room. Glancing at the mantel clock, he figured he had maybe half-an-hour before the two inspectors showed up.

As fast as his aged body could manage it, he changed into traveling clothes, opened the safe then jammed cash, diamonds and jewelry into a small suitcase. Fifteen minutes had elapsed by the time he was in his car, an older Bentley, driving down the driveway, pressing the garage door remote to close the door.

He was though the main gate to the neighborhood, passing the parked sedan of the two inspectors who stood at the security hut, talking to the guard who gave Mark a wave and a grin before returning his attention to the two men. One of the men, Nichols turned back to study the car then turned back.

Mark looked in his rearview mirror, suddenly nervous when he saw Callahan and Nichols race to their sedan and turn it around in front of the gate. Mark immediately turned on the first street and for the next hour, wove his way through streets and byways until he was out on the open road, heading west.

Everyday folks were at work by the time he approached Lexington, Kentucky. Deciding now was the time for a new vehicle, he pressed the button on his dash, activating the directions program.

"Luxury vehicles, Lexington, Kentucky."

"There are eight locations offering luxury autos in Lexington. Please refine your search."

Mark thought for a moment and smiled. No one would be looking for him driving a truck. Giving the program new instructions, Mark soon pulled into a dealership. After much haggling, Mark settled at an even swap for a Ford F-150 Platinum Super Cab.

Three hours later, Mark was cheerily heading west once again. Giving thought to his predicament, he wondered if it wasn't time to leave the country, settle overseas for a spell. He could fly out of Denver. Yes, Chicago was closer, but there was no rush now, especially as he had lost his pursuers.

For several days, Mark drove like an old man, observing the speed limits while his heart went to his throat each time he saw a policeman on the side of the road or passing him on the highway. He found himself easily tiring and each time he stopped for meals, the waitresses all treated him with the overt sweetness of helping their grandfather.

By the time he reached Denver, he found he had spent more time resting than driving. At first he thought it was the stress of the escape and pursuit, but the truth was, he wasn't sleeping well and he was always tired.

Frustrated, he abruptly decided that he didn't want to fly out of Denver, that he would head west and fly out somewhere along the coast. Then the quirky idea of seeing the Grand Canyon emerged. He had never seen it before and never had the urge to take the time to see it.

Why now?

He shrugged at the curious thought then smiled. Why not? It wasn't like he had to get somewhere by a specific time. In fact, the more time he took, the likelihood Callahan and Nichols would believe he fled the country.

He chuckled at the thought and continued on through the city, driving on I-70 following the signs to Vegas. By the time he got to Grand Junction, he was struggling to stay awake. Searching the dashboard, he pressed the button activating the directions program.

"Hotels with suites, Grand Junction, Colorado."

"There are twenty-one hotels listed with suites."

"Five-star hotel."

"There are no five star hotels in Grand Junction, Colorado."

"Four-star hotels."

"There are no four-star hotels in Grand Junction, Colorado."

"What?" Mark frowned in frustration. He was so tired and he had half a mind to pull over and doze for a few minutes, but he knew that would only attract unwanted attention.

"There are no four-star hotels in Grand Junction, Colorado."

"Three-star hotels, with suites," he sighed.

"There are nine hotels with suites in Grand Junction, Colorado."

"Pick one, damn it."

"I'm sorry, but I did not understand your last request."

"Most expensive hotels with suites."

"There are two hotels at the same price, the Hampton Inn and the Springhill Suites. They are in the downtown district of Grand Junction."

"Springhill Suites."

"Take exit thirty-seven which is four point three miles ahead."

Mark followed the voice directions and finally arrived at the hotel, checked in and was soon stretched out asleep on the king-sized bed.

It was dark when he awoke and he startled trying to remember where he was. Calming himself, he thought back to the last thing he remembered, which was loading the car and leaving the house then eluding Callahan and Nichols.

Visions of landscapes from the trip west coalesced and then he abruptly remembered checking into the hotel.

"What the hell is happening to me?" he mumbled, pushing himself to sit on the edge of the bed, noticing the clock on the nightstand by the bed, the red iridescent numbers giving a dull light and telling him it was 7:45 p.m.

Finding the light switch, he flicked it on, found the remote and turned on the TV. As the sound came on, he ignored the station and shuffled to the bathroom, flipping the light switch to stare in the mirror.

What stared back was an old man who had slept in his clothes. He leaned forward to study his face then slowly raised his hands to focus on the age spots, wrinkles, and gnarled fingers then back to numbly stare at the reflection of his face.

His body ached and the grinding of his joints seemed to have sounds. A sad epiphany occurred and his eyes misted as he uttered a long and resigned sigh.

He was dying.

He stayed in Grand Junction for another two weeks, early on muddling up and down Main Street as far as his decrepit legs and mind could stand. Most days he stayed in the hotel room, the TV on to no particular channel while he sat staring out the window to the mountains in the distance or slept only to awaken in the early morning hours with the TV blaring infomercials.

When he did venture out to a café or restaurant, he could see the looks in their eyes, an overt pity mixed with relief that they had years of life still remaining. By the fourth day, he hated their looks, their pity, and stayed in the hotel room rather than face their condescending false interest and charity.

After the fourth time of counting and marveling at the cache of diamonds, he lost interest and tucked them away. By the sixth day, he remained at the window, staring out to watch as life passed by him. Meals were delivered by local restaurants and the remains collected by the cleaning staff.

At the end of two weeks, he was ready. Collecting his things, he paid his bill and once again headed west, stopping for the night in Salina, Utah.

He was up early the next morning, well before dawn, stopping in Marysvale for breakfast at the Prospector Café. It was as he was enjoying his sausage and biscuits that a young man came in, a rancher by the look of him who greeted the owners like a regular.

Noting Mark was the only customer in the place, he amiably smiled. "That your truck?"

"Yes it is." Mark smiled back.

"Nice truck."

"Thank you."

The man studied him a bit then said, "If you don't mind me saying, old timer, you don't seem to be the pick-up type."

"I'm not," Mark replied debating whether he wanted conversation or not, especially after being called 'old timer.'

The man chuckled and sat down at a table close to Mark. "Where ya headed?"

"I'm going to take a look at the Grand Canyon." Mark finished off the last piece of sausage.

"Ah," he nodded. "Been there a couple of times. Even did some hiking there. You'll enjoy it."

Mark politely smiled when an idea struck him that caused his smile to widen. "So what are you driving?"

"Nothing like that," he chuckled with envy. "Thanks Betty," he said as the waitress deposited a plate of pancakes with three eggs over easy on top, a cup of coffee and a small bowl of creamers. Opening up three of the creamers, he poured them into his coffee. "I got a ten-year-old Dodge Ram 1500."

"Tell you the truth," Mark confided. "I know nothing about trucks. I traded my Bentley for the one outside thinking it might be fun to try something different. And it is sort of fun being up so high when you're driving. Almost makes you feel like you 're in an eighteen-wheeler."

The man paused mid-chew. "You traded a Bentley for a pickup truck?"

"Yes. The dealer was rather pleased with the trade. I had less than twenty thousand miles on the Bentley. Of course, the truck is brand new."

"Jeez, mister, what do you do?"

"I'm an independent investment analyst." He chuckled after he said it for it sounded impressive.

The man stared blankly at him. "What does an independent investment analyst do?"

"I make money for myself investing in various commodities, securities, and tangibles."

"Tangibles?"

"Things like diamonds, precious stones, gold, or even watches like this." He held up his arm to display the Rolex.

"Looks like you've done pretty good for yourself," the man said with admiration.

Mark noted the man's reaction. While the man was impressed, he wasn't envious in that overt way that said he was jealous of another man's success. The man seemed far too content with what he had, and that puzzled Mark.

"Here." Mark unclipped the watch and held it out to the man. "You can have it."

The man arched an eyebrow. "You're giving me your watch?"

"Yes."

"Why would you want to give me your watch?"

Mark shrugged. "Because I feel like it."

"But I've already got a watch and it works just fine." He held up his arm, displaying the inexpensive watch. "It's a Timex and I guarantee it'll keep time just as good as that watch you got there, for a whole lot less than you spent on that one."

Mark frowned in surprise. "You don't want this watch?"

The man placed his knife on the side of his plate. "Now what would I do with a watch like that? It's not like I'm gonna wear it while I'm working. Most likely it would sit in the top drawer of my dresser, taking up space."

"You really don't want it?"

"No thanks."

"Do over."

The inside of the Prospector Café whirled and settled, with Mark holding up his arm.

"You can have it."

The man arched an eyebrow. "You're giving me your watch?"

"Yes."

"Why would you want to give me your watch?"

The scene played out like before and did so six more times. By the last time, it was an exhausting effort holding up his arm.

Mark suddenly worried that he wouldn't make it to the Grand Canyon.

"What's your name?"

"Luke," the man replied, slicing up his pancakes and eggs.

"I've got a proposition for you, Luke. As you can see, I'm not a spritely young man anymore. I tire easily. I'm looking for someone to drive me to the Grand Canyon. I'll pay you for it."

"You want me to drive you to the Grand Canyon?"

"Yes. Just for today. We can take my truck. We go there, spend an hour or two then come right back. I'll pay you twice what you would make today. Three times."

Luke placed his fork and knife on the side of the plate then peered intently at Mark. "You'll pay me to drive you down to see the Grand Canyon."

"You'll be gone only for today."

Luke gave him a bemused smile. "OK. Once we finish breakfast, I'll take you there."

"Do you need to let your employer know?"

"I own my ranch. It's not much, but we get by. I'll let my wife know I'll be gone for a while."

"How much do I owe you?"

Luke grinned at him. "Mister –"

"My name's Mark."

"Mark, I don't need your money. I'm quite content with what I got, especially the wife and kids. I'm doing this because you look like a man who could use a friend."

Mark blinked at the revelation, turning his head away so that Luke would not see his eyes mist.

Luke pulled into an almost deserted parking lot at the North Rim Lodge.

"Thank you for a most enjoyable trip," Mark said. "You are a wonderful travelling companion."

"Thank you, Mark. You're not so bad yourself," he teased.

"Sorry," Mark said with a limp smile, knowing he had slept a good portion of the trip.

Luke started to open his door when Mark stopped him.

"If you don't mind, I'd like to go by myself. It's hard to explain, but I need to be alone."

"Of course," Luke replied with a kind smile. "I'll just wait for you here."

"Thanks."

Mark emerged from the truck, took his bearing and started his methodical shuffle along Bright Angel Point Trail. The day was chilly though filled with bright sunshine. By the time he reached the end, the few early visitors had walked back.

Oblivious to several vultures, wings stretched wide, riding the thermals in large circles high above him, Mark stood at the guardrail, staring out across the distances to the far canyon walls. Yet his body ached, and he was tired with the lethargy of ennui. Even the beauty of the day held no value to him.

"I thought I'd find you here," a voice behind him said.

Mark looked over his shoulder then frowned in surprise. "You. Where have you been all this time?"

"Watching you grow old," Nathan replied, walking up to stand beside him. He studied how Mark stood, bent over, his hand in his pocket.

"I see you still have the stone I gave you."

Mark fingered the worn stone in his pocket. "Yes."

Nathan placed his hands on the railing and looked around at the rocks and far walls. "You've changed. I almost didn't recognize you."

"I don't recognize myself," he scoffed. "What's happened to me?"

"You weren't as responsible as I thought you might be."

"What's that supposed to mean?"

"It means that I had hoped you wouldn't make the same mistakes I did."

Mark glared at him, splaying his arms. "Look at me. I look like I'm 80 years old."

"Choices have consequences," the man said.

"To hell with your choices and consequences," Mark snapped. "Why am I like this?"

Nathan paused, looked briefly at Mark then turned his attention to the canyon. "Every time you use the stone, part of your time is taken. You can't play with time and not expect consequences."

"Why don't you look as old as I do?"

"Because I recognized what was happening and knew the only way to stop it was to get rid of the stone."

Mark inhaled a pained sigh that morphed to resigned fate. "Was it hard?"

"Look at me. I look like I'm 50 years old. I'm only 33."

"Hell, you're older than I am," Mark said, shaking his head.

Nathan shrugged then held out his hand. "Are you ready to give the stone to someone else?"

Mark withdrew the smooth stone that he had carried for what seemed his whole life. "Here." He dropped it into Nathan's palm. "It won't do me any good anymore."

"Are you sure?"

"I'm dying."

"That's a pity."

Mark sniffed with disdain. "Yeah, but not for you." He looked up at the narrow rock formation immediately behind them. He had seen some teenagers gamboling on the top and gauged whether he could make the climb.

Nathan saw his glance. "A wise decision. I'll help you."

"One thing first," Mark said holding up a hand. "There's a young man... Hell, he's probably our age. Anyway, there's a young man named Luke in a Ford F-150 Platinum Super Cab. I want him to have my truck and everything in it."

"OK."

"Promise," Mark demanded.

"Rest assured, my friend, it will be as you wish."

"Give him this too." He took off his watch and handed it to Nathan.

It was a slow struggle, but Mark finally made it to the top of the rocks, his vertigo wreaking havoc as he forced himself to stand then look over the sheer drop to rocks below. Nathan had detached himself before the top and was standing below on the pathway.

Mark stood wavering as he looked down with sad eyes. Turning around, he inhaled a deep breath one last time, then raised his head, closed his eyes, lifted his arms and fell backwards.

Nathan walked over to the railing to watch him fall then disappear to the rocks below. Holding the stone in his hand, he returned to the parking lot and tapped on the window where Luke sat listening to the radio.

Luke pressed the switch and powered down the window. "Yes?"

"You're waiting for Mark?"

"Yes."

"He won't be coming back."

"Why not?"

"He was at the end of his life," Nathan said with forced gravitas. "You were very kind to bring him here."

Understanding punched through Luke and he grabbed the door handle. Nathan placed a hand on the door stopping him.

"Don't bother. He's gone."

"Who are you?"

"A friend. I've been waiting for him. He said that he wanted you to have this truck and everything in it. And this too," Nathan said, holding up the watch.

Luke frowned in confusion as he accepted the watch.

"Mark also said that you looked like a responsible man and wanted you to have this." He held out the stone for Luke to see.

"A rock?"

"A stone," Nathan corrected. "A 'Do Over' stone."

"What's a 'do over' stone?"

"It's a stone that lets you make changes to the past, like Ctrl Z."

"Ctrl Z?"

With a winning smile, Nathan said, "On the computer keyboard. You simply hold the one key down then press the

'Z' key and poof, you get rid of what you don't like and can start all over again."